Cursed With a Twist
by
Constance Barker

Sign up for Constance Barker's New Releases Newsletter

Chapter One

Ginger

The clock approached twelve p.m. and the hot grill and cold drinks awaited customers. I wiped the tables one last time in anticipation of the lunch crowd. Dad was in the back pretending to help Bones with the food and Dixie worked the bar. We were ready for another day at The Grumpy Chicken.

Digger crawled into the pub, maybe weary from hard work or as a display of his mood. Most days he was predictable, but today it was ten minutes till noon when he plunked on his usual bar stool. Dixie approached him and asked, "Slow day in the dirt and shovel business? You're twenty minutes early."

He winced. "Ha. Ha. So funny — not! I'll have you know it's mostly maintenance work, not digging. The place needs to be mowed and cleaned, too. And in this small town, it's not like we bury someone every day."

Dixie chuckled. "I know. I'm just messing with ya."

Another routine day in the pub and the boredom of it delighted me because my unusual days were worse than a fender bender or spilled coffee. My off days involved things like thieves, murderers, psychics, and yes, even ghost chickens. This casual banter was music to my ears. It was normal.

I asked, "Why are you early today, Digger?"

"Got everything nice and tidy at the cemetery and I found something I wanted to show to the gang. See if it means anything to anyone."

I wrinkled my forehead."That sounds interesting, what is it?"

Digger sighed and gave me a stern look. "Well, to be honest, Ginger, you should see it first. I found it on your Mom's headstone."

"What, did someone defile it?"

Digger chuckled and shook his head no. "Relax, nothing like that. Let me show you." He plunged his hand into one of the many pockets of his overalls. When he produced a fist holding the contents, my normal day ended.

The lights buzzed like electricity within struggled to escape the glass bulb confinement and bright white light blazed from every fixture. A blast of cold air ruffled my hair and my ears caught the howl of an odd whoosh on the counter behind the bar. After the rare gust of indoor wintry wind, a supernatural thumping from a rhythm-challenged poltergeist thundered from the floor, vibrating the glasses on the bar. The grumpy chicken was at it again.

When it stopped, Dixie exclaimed, "Son of an icicle! Not the pickled egg jar again! Doesn't this bleeping ghost chicken know how to mess with something else!"

I spun to check my pickled eggs. This particular jar in this specific pub was in constant peril. We went through nine jars in the last year and all found the same shattered end on the floor. However, this time I observed a jar of frozen pickled eggs covered on the outside with frost. Fog rose off the frigid apothecary jar and without warning, it popped. I witnessed hairline cracks rippling through the ice-encrusted glass.

"Well, that's not normal." Digger froze, still concealing the item in his fist as he spoke.

Dixie grabbed a bucket and plunged the frozen jar into a bucket. "At least this time it's solid and easy to clean up. But when that melts it's gonna be a mess."

"What was that all about?" I scanned the area to see if anything else needed attention.

Digger mumbled, "It's cold. Real cold."

Dixie whined, "Speak up. And we know the eggs froze."

"No, this." Digger opened his fist to reveal a small heart-shaped locket and fog rose off the gold necklace.

"That's what caused all this? And it was on my Mom's headstone?" I have observed enough to understand when the grumpy chicken was acting up. And this little locket upset our white feathered, paranormal friend.

Digger nodded. "Yes. It was just sitting there, glinting in the sun like it was calling to me."

Dad and Bones rushed through the swinging door from the kitchen. Dad demanded, "What was all that thumping?"

I shrugged. "Not sure. Trying to figure it out."

Dixie added, "It was the chicken throwing a fit."

Digger nodded in agreement. "Dixie's right. And it happened when I took this out of my pocket." He held up the gold necklace for all to view.

"Can I see it?" The gold locket drew me and I needed to touch it.

"Sure. There's an inscription on the back and pictures inside it." Digger extended his hand.

I took the pretty piece of jewelry and examined it. It appeared old and on the back it read 'To my love Erin Byrne.' I asked, "Does this name mean anything to you, Digger?"

"Nope."

"It's beautiful. I can't believe it was just sitting out in the open." I ran my fingers over the etched decorations on the front.

"Me neither. But it was." Digger pointed at it. "Open it up."

I found the clasp and flipped it open. Two black and white pictures stared back at me, one of a man and the other a woman. "Digger, do you recognize these two people?"

"Nope. But the woman looks a bit like you."

I huffed. "Nooo. You're imagining things."

Digger leaned on the bar. "Well, it's a big coincidence finding it on your Mom's grave, sure. But she looks a little like you."

The front door swung open and Piper strutted in followed by Ida. "How's it going at the best watering hole in Potter's Mill? Ida and I just ordered some great stuff online."

We all stared at the two internet shoppers till Dixie shot back, "Well, while you were spending money on some bauble or trinket, you missed the grumper messing with things again."

Ida made a long face. "Aw, did we miss anything cool?"

"Real cool, literally. A frozen pickle jar that broke from the pressure of the ice inside...Lights buzzed and they got real bright...Then it sounded like an invisible giant tried to dance on the floor. Shook the bar." Dixie pointed to each location as she described the events.

Piper tilted her head a little. "That's different. The lights usually dim with no sound."

Ida squinted at me. "What caused all that?"

I held up the locket. "I think this."

"It's so pretty. Can I see." Piper moved over to the bar and took a seat. I closed the locket and handed it to her. "Ginger, this looks really old." Piper turned it multiple times to inspect the piece.

"I thought the same thing. And the pictures inside look old too."

The front entry hinges creaked again and we all turned to see Star, the owner of the new age shop next door. She entered but crept into the dining room, stopping ten feet from the bar. "Something happened, didn't it? I feel a disturbance."

Dixie snorted. "You could say that."

Dad added, "It's been a while since our plucky phantom hen has made her presence known. Glad she did, it's good for our business."

Star finished her walk to the bar and sat on a stool. "Did anything special happen to cause it."

I grabbed the locket from Piper. "This seems to be the source." I gave it to her.

Star took it, and as she grasped it, I regretted handing it to her. She flinched, like a jolt of electricity flowed through her. Mysterious, muted thunder cracked from nowhere in particular, or perhaps from another plane of existence. Star sank into her stool and her head drooped to her chest with eyes closed, for an instant. And then she sat up straight, picked her head up, and opened her eyes. "I sense multiple spirits and they are trying to communicate with us. This locket is part of a message."

Digger raised his voice. "Star, I found it on Jessica O'Mallory's headstone. Does that mean anything?"

Star's gaze cut through the old gravedigger. "Maybe. When did you find it?"

"This morning."

Star turned to make eye contact with me. "These spirits need to tell you something. But I'm not sure what it is. And you should know, what these other entities want to communicate worries the grumpy chicken."

Dixie raised her eyebrows. "Well, there's something you don't hear every day."

Piper cut in, "Ya know, if it's part of some sort of message, from my time as a journalist in Atlanta, I might know someone who can help us. This locket seems really old and the man I'm thinking of works in the state historical society. He might be able to find out who this Erin Byrne is and get us information about who the family was. And maybe he can tell something about the jewelry, who made it and so on."

I rubbed my forehead. "Atlanta is a ways from here and does he really need to examine it in person? Or can we just email some pictures? I would rather not part with it."

Piper smiled. "Maybe we don't have to. First, Atlanta is only a few hours away. Second, you know I was planning on visiting Atlanta tomorrow, to visit some old friends, including Jayson. During my visit, I can pop over to the historical society and show it to the experts. Let them examine it, up close, so it's more likely they discover something. Then bring it back. It never has to leave my possession."

I groaned. "First, that old boyfriend of yours was never right for you. And second, the historical society is a good idea, but I would feel better if you kept it with you at all times."

Piper frowned. "You're worse than my father. You never like any of my boyfriends."

"I'm not judging." I raised my hands in surrender and took a step back.

Star interrupted. "This locket has a strong aura. I would keep it close. It may have more value than anyone suspects."

Digger spoke with confidence. "I found it. And I want to go with Piper to help. Make sure the thing stays safe."

Piper tittered. "Ah, no, no, no. I can do it alone."

Digger glared at her. "I insist. I found it, so technically

it's mine."

Ida nudged Piper. "He's got ya there."

Piper snapped back at Ida. "Button it. You're not helping."

Digger continued, "Look, I know I'm not Ginger or Ida and I'm not going to be able to chat about the latest girly things in the car, but I need to go and make sure this find of mine stays safe."

Ida scrunched her nose at Digger. "I wonder what you consider to be girly things we chat about?"

Digger blushed. "Ya know. I don't want to talk about it."

Piper laughed. "OK, it should prove to be an interesting ride, but I can use some company on the drive and I think I can handle the girly free chat. But you'll be on your own when Jayson and I go to lunch. And we leave early in the morning."

Digger nodded in thanks. "No problem, I can take the day off tomorrow. Someone needs to keep the locket safe while you're out carousing like a jet-setter in the big city."

I added, "So it's decided. Let's see what the historians can tell us."

Digger and Piper nodded to each other to confirm the plan. And with that, everyone ordered lunch.

Chapter Two

Dixie

The large wooden bar is an integral part of the pub and is a continual mess because of the constant use. Tom and Ginger work hard, but they deal with food or other things most of the time. As the bartender, my job is to clean and organize the lounge area and ensure the customers have fresh drinks. It is hard work, but satisfying. I must find something in it because I have worked here for thirty years, since being a young twenty-something.

Guardrail wandered in with Dog Breath in tow and they took their usual spots at the bar. Guardrail bellowed, "Good day pretty ladies." He gave Ida and me a slight bow with his head, then continued, "One beer and one pickled egg, Dixie, s'il vous plait."

I snorted at the big motorcycle mechanic. "I can get ya the beer. But didn't you hear? The jar went to chicken heaven again. This time by ice."

"Why does the egg jar always have to be what gets broken!" He smacked the bar top and scanned the dining room and bar like he was looking for a lost stress relief toy. "Where's Ginger?"

Ida was sitting at the bar and answered, "Getting ready in the apartment. I'm waiting for her. We plan on scoping out town today and see what she can learn about the gold locket."

Dog pinched his eyebrows. "What locket?"

I laughed. "You boys missed a lot, should've been here yesterday. Star went into one of her freakish trances. And a mysterious locket made the chicken go wacko, which resulted in freezing the pickled egg jar solid." I poured and served two beers to them while I spoke.

Guardrail whined as he took the beer, "We had a big job to get done and worked all day and night yesterday. Of course we were working when all the interesting stuff was happening over here."

Dog shook his head. "Well, no one can say this place is dull."

Ida threw out, "Hey, either of you ever heard of Erin Byrne?"

They shook their heads no. Guardrail asked, "No, why? Who is she?"

Ida shifted on her stool to better view the boys. "It's the name inscribed on the back of the mystery locket. Me and Ginger are planning on asking around today.

See if anyone knows the name. And there are two pictures inside the locket. One of a man and another of a woman. The lady looks a little like Ginger."

"Really? Can I see?" Dog alternated his glance back and forth from Ida to me.

Ida answered, "Sure, I got pics on my phone of the inside and outside of it."

Dog Breath grabbed his beer and moved over to a seat next to Ida. He extended his hand to her. "If you don't mind?" Ida took out her fancy phone, opened the picture files, and handed the expensive electronic gizmo to him. Dog pawed at the screen to examine the images and gasped when got to the picture of the woman in the locket. "Dang, she does look like Ginger. But you ya know what, this guy also looks a little like Elias Holland."

Ginger bounded down the stairs from the apartment over the pub. Her pretty red hair was down, not in the usual pony tail, and flowed in the passing air as she descended. She hollered on her way to the bar, "Hey Dixie! I'm ready to go check around town with Ida and see if someone knows about this locket. Can you hold the fort down?"

I answered, "Sure."

Ida snatched her phone from Dog. "I'm going to need this, sorry."

Ginger took a stool at the bar, next to Ida. "I really

appreciate when you cover for me, Dixie."

"You're welcome. But you're lucky that you have a superhero bartender that does it all while you snoop about town." I was always glad to help the O'Mallorys, they are family to me. Ginger is younger than me, like a little sister, but I learn and grow as a person with her in my life. For example, after my divorce, I was alone, raising three kids. To cope, I began drinking extra wine and swearing like a contractor. Tom chastised my cussing at work for years and made me put money in a curse jar whenever I offended, but it failed to stop me and the glass vessel swallowed many of my tips. Two years ago, though, Ginger had an idea. We made a mutual new year's resolution to stop swearing. It took the pact with Ginger to break the habit and afterward I realized it worked because I feared to disappoint her. And deep down, I may have wanted to emulate her. Besides, I learned how fun it is to invent new non-swear cuss words. Except for that one time I slipped with "Flash Gordon's nipples." The gang still teases me for that one.

Ida put her phone away and said to me, "Talk to ya later, Dixie. Don't let the Hardly Boys over there keep you from your work."

"I think I know how to deal with my regulars. Happy sleuthing and good luck." I respect Ginger, but my gut told me she was on a snipe hunt with this one. However, she is intelligent and tenacious and no one should underestimate her, especially me.

Bones burst from the kitchen. "Ginger, wait! I want to

go with you. I'm always stuck in the kitchen and miss out on the action. Digger got to go to Atlanta. Let me help you today."

Ginger hemmed and hawed then said, "Alright, if Dad will cover the grill. But there may be work waiting for you to catch-up on when we get back. If you can deal with that, you can come."

Bones' noggin rocked like a bobble head. "Yes, I'll take care of whatever piles up while we're gone."

Tom shouted from the kitchen. "That's good. Because I'm the owner of this place and there is no way I'm washing pans!"

Ginger smiled. "What did I tell you, I know my Dad. You're lucky he likes you or he wouldn't do the cooking to cover for ya."

I added, "Better be careful Bones. Tom may take a liking to the grill and put you out of work."

Bones waved me off with one hand and Tom's voice bellowed from the kitchen again. "No danger of that, Dixie. I prefer to drink beer and talk with the customers. And Ginger, don't take too long or my good mood may evaporate."

Dog mumbled, "This is his good mood?"

Bones' eyes drooped. "I better go make sure everything is caught up before we leave. Please wait, just a minute." Ginger nodded in agreement and he sprinted back into the kitchen.

Ginger glanced at me. "The air in here feels calm since Piper and Digger headed for Atlanta this morning. You think the chicken is quiet because the locket is gone?"

I glanced around the bar. "I don't know. But you're right, it feels peaceful since they left."

While waiting for Bones, Ginger picked up and bent a plastic stir stick into a pretzel. After a minute she asked, "What do you think Star meant when she said the grumpy chicken is worried about what these other spirits wanted to communicate?" She did not address anyone in particular.

I shrugged. "I don't know. Star says lots of weird stuff. I've learned to just let it roll off my back and not fixate on it. Just like most of what is said in this place."

Ginger chuckled. "I guess that is a good trait for a bartender." She threw the bent piece of plastic on the bar. "But Star has always been right when she gets that weird expression. Her voice even becomes softer and kind of eerie. You can tell she really sensed something."

Ida added, "I know it spooked me. I don't like the idea of ghosts trying to tell us something. And the prospect of a concerned chicken ghost is not good." Ida chuckled, then continued, "I can't believe I live in a town where saying things like that make sense."

I cleaned some glasses, then said, "What about this. Maybe these other spirits want to move in on the pub, Kick the chicken out and make it their home. I hope not, I'm just getting used to the pain in the feathers. But maybe the new ghost tenants won't break things like the ol' grumper."

Guardrail interjected, "I'd like that. I'd have pickled eggs to eat then."

Ginger shook her head. "No, that's not something they 'know' or want to communicate. What you described is a turf war. And that's not what Star said."

Ida added, "Yeah, Star said they wanted to *tell* you something."

Dog asked, "Well, what could a spirit know to tell about another spirit? And in particular, a chicken ghost?"

Ginger mulled. "You know that brings up some questions I've been chewing on. Who is the grumpy chicken and where did it come from? Why is it here?"

I laughed. "Some things just seem right. Even though she freaks me out with most of the antics, this place has always been home to the grumpy chicken. So I never really thought about that. It feels right."

Ginger's face grew stern. "If we knew a little more about who our chicken spirit is, why it's here and not someplace else, maybe we would better understand why some other spirits are trying to send us a message concerning her."

"Good luck with that one. I'm not sure you can just look up information about a chicken spirit on Facebook." I looked at Ginger sideways, the way you do when someone proposes a far fetched idea.

Ginger ignored me and continued. "That's why I want to ask around town today, Dixie. The grumpy chicken is part of Potter's Mill history. I'm willing to bet someone knows a legend or some obscure story that can help us connect the locket and the grumpy chicken."

Ida threw out, "Well, did you ask your Dad? He seems like the first one to ask."

Ginger chuckled. "I did. He said it didn't matter as long she stays put and sells souvenirs."

Tom hollered from the kitchen, "That's all ya need to know. Stop making a souffle out of a potato."

I flinched. "What in the world does that mean, old man?"

Ginger smiled. "You're surprised to hear an Irishman relate to potatoes?"

Tom bellowed from the kitchen. "Ya know what I mean, Dixie. Sometimes a potato is just a potato. Stop poking into the grumper's story. Leave it alone."

I snorted. "That clears it up, Tom. Thanks."

Bones pushed open the swinging door and came into the dining room. He had combed his hair and put on a clean shirt. "Ready to go. Let's do this!"

Ginger laughed at his energy, rose off her stool, and made for the front door with Bones and Ida. They were chattering about something as they exited. Tom came out into the dining room and walked over to me at the bar. He seemed restless. "I don't like this, I tell ya. She shouldn't be spending so much time on that silly locket thing. She might not like what she finds."

I exhaled. "You're overprotective of her sometimes. Especially when it comes to the history of this place. At some point, you have to tell her the whole story. She can handle it."

Tom sighed. "I know. But she's my little girl."

"She's all grown up, married and divorced, solved crimes, including murder. And she deals with you every day. I think she's tough enough to know the real history of The Grumpy Chicken."

"That's not it. Her mother knew things. She always said that when Ginger knows who she really is, where she came from, it will change her forever."

"I hate when you say creepy stuff like that."

Tom sighed. "It is no coincidence that this necklace was found on my wife's headstone. I can feel it in me bones. Jessica is still trying to help me and Ginger."

"And how is it helping?"

"Right now, I don't know. It's a mystery and we'll have to wait and see."

"Do you know something you're not telling me, old man?"

"Nope. But like you said, Dixie, I'm old and may have forgotten things." He smiled at me like a big brother who just took a lollipop from his little sister.

"Jeez, sorry. I'm just your bartender and I can be a little pushy. I know. But I raised three kids on my own, so I have an excuse." After a pause, I added, "But I do care about you and Ginger and will do whatever I can to help you both."

Tom lowered his head and chuckled. "A little pushy? More like a lot. But I know you care, and I appreciate it." He took a deep breath to collect his thoughts. "This is all happening too soon for me and I'm powerless to do anything. I don't want to think about this anymore."

He turned and went through the swinging door into the kitchen. After a few seconds, from the back of the cook-room the office door clacked shut. Tom hid a special bottle of single-malt Jameson in one of the desk drawers and I was certain he went to commiserate with it.

Chapter Three

Edith

The general store took so long to get my knitting materials, but I wanted to give the business to Freddie Warner. It was proper to help our local merchants when you could. My sister Lily disagreed, but she could buy her things her way and I bought mine my way.

We have lived together our whole lives and Lily and I never managed to marry. But back in our younger days, the boys loved to chase us and we dated our fair share of eligible bachelors. We loved to have fun, especially if it involved motorcycles. One time I took off on Jimmy Parker's prized Indian motorcycle. He ran down the street behind me cussing a blue streak. I laughed the entire time. Suffice it to say it was the last time I ever rode on JP's bike. Our antics also upset our father, a career military man. He was strict, but we loved him to death and he would do anything to make us happy.

Everyone in our family pushed us to get hitched, but

we were having too much fun and the years passed. As we grew older, age forced us to settle down and we started to enjoy some of the simpler things in life, including each other's company. A portrait of Dad watches over us now. Life is funny that way and it's just how it turned out for the two of us.

One of my orders was in, so I walked over to the general store to retrieve it. I needed the yarn to work on a sweater I was making for my nephew stationed in Germany. Freddie was attentive as usual and went in back to get my package, so I waited by strolling the aisles to search for anything new or on sale. Ginger, Ida, and Bones came in with a burst of energy. Ginger said, "Good afternoon, Edith. Nice to see you today."

I put down the pregnancy test. "Nice to see you too."

Ida blurted out, "You expecting?"

I huffed at her silliness. "At my age? Heavens no. We didn't have things like this when I was young. And it was on sale. I was curious, just checking it out." I noted Bones blushing.

Ginger said, "Let's *please* change the subject, if I can. We're checking around for information and spotted you in here, thought you might help us. We need to learn about a woman named Erin Byrnes. You ever hear that name?"

I blinked a few times. "No, I don't think so. Maybe Lily has. She knows the lineage of the townsfolk better than me."

Freddie Warner came out of the stock room with my package and said, "Well hello. When did the crowd show up?"

Ida answered, "Hello Freddie, we're not shopping. Sorry. We're poking around town asking about an Erin Byrnes. You ever hear that name?"

Freddie replied, "No, not Erin. But Byrnes was a family way back when that helped to start this town. Just after the civil war ended"

That tweaked my memory. "Ya know, I think I have heard Lily talk about the civil war and the Byrnes name, now that you say that."

Ginger asked, "Did they have anything to do with the tavern?"

I shrugged. "I don't know. Why do you ask, dear?"

Ginger sighed, then answered. "Something strange happened yesterday. A locket with the name Erin Byrnes inscribed on the back made the grumpy chicken act up. Star says it was because the locket is part of a message other spirits are trying to communicate to us and it worried the grumper."

"Dang! Lily and I missed it. We decided to stay in yesterday." The chicken spirit could be spooky, but it was so exhilarating to experience its presence. Lily would be upset, too, for missing the excitement.

Ginger added, "It was pretty empty in the pub when it happened, so just about everyone missed it. Don't feel bad."

I said, "Ya know, speaking of the Civil War, I've heard all kinds of ghost stories associated with the war. And you do have a ghost chicken."

Ida laughed. "That's a thin connection."

I persisted. "But when did the pub start? Just after the war, right?"

Ginger nodded. "Yes, I believe so."

Bones was antsy and burst. "Well, what kind of ghost stories were told during the war? Anything like the grumpy chicken?"

I snickered. "No. I don't know any chicken ghosts from the civil war. But weird things happened all the time back then."

Freddie cut in, "Edith, tell them about Shiloh. That story always spooked me as a kid."

I took a deep breath. "Well, during the Battle of Shiloh, thousands of soldiers were injured and left lying in mud for days. While waiting for help, some of the injured noticed that many of the wounds glowed green in the dark. And even more strange, when they were finally taken to the sorely lacking field hospitals, those who had green glowing wounds had better survival rates. So the troops starting calling the event "Angels' Glow.""

Bones shivered. "Angels' Glow, that's so creepy. That

can't be true."

"I can check that out easy enough. Let's see what the internet has to say." Ida took her phone out and did a quick search.

Ginger said, "So that's interesting, but Shiloh is in Tennessee. This is Georgia."

Ida popped, "Well, seems that there is lots of stuff about Angels' Glow at Shiloh. It really happened."

I laughed. "I told you. You're all too young to know most of them, but, there are all kinds of ghost stories from the Civil War. And Ginger, sweetie, Georgia does have its fair share."

Freddie added, "I heard that the old cemetery has ghost sightings every now and then, mostly near or on the anniversary of Sherman passing through here on his March to the Sea."

I said, "As a little girl, Lily once saw a woman in a long, flowing white night gown at the old church. She was floating in the air and Lily could see straight through her."

Ginger's eye grew, slightly. "That's kind of a coincidence. Digger found this locket on my Mom's headstone. That's the new cemetery, but it's just across from the old cemetery. And right next to the old church"

I wondered, "Did you find this locket you mentioned, dear?" Ginger shook her head no, so I asked, "Well who did?"

"Digger." Ginger tilted her head back after answering me.

Freddie asked, "Is there any significance to who found it?"

"That's a good question. And Star asked the same question yesterday. Maybe?" Ida put her phone away as she replied.

Ginger said, "Maybe we should be going. We were actually on our way to town hall when we saw you in here, Edith. Bones here has bravely offered to go see Abbey there, see if she will let us go through some of the archives they have."

Freddie scrunched up his face. "Why is that brave of Bones."

I laughed. "Did you forget already, Freddie? Bones went on a date with her while living with another girl."

Ida chuckled. "Bones proved it's impossible to date two women at the same time in a small town."

Freddie laughed. "I remember now. Didn't she throw you out for it?"

Bones hung his head. "Yeah, slept in my car for a week, but we got back together. So it is kind of pushing it for me to go to town hall. But she's the clerk there and we need to see the archives. And I know Abbey better than anyone else from the pub."

Ginger smiled. "Thanks, Edith, Freddie, but we should

be off. We need to make the rounds. See ya around."

Freddie and I waved goodbye. The trio left with the same burst energy as when they arrived. After the front door closed, tinkling the bell on the door as it did whenever the door moved, Freddie said, "Byrnes was the family that did a lot to get this town established, they should find something in the archives."

I smiled at the shopkeeper, "My memory is too frail at seventy-three to remember who started Potter's Mill, but I'm pretty sure if there is something to find, Ginger will find it. She has proved to be a good detective."

Freddie added, "Well, she better be careful. If she is stirring up old history, going back to the war, people may get upset. That was a bad time and changed the lives of everybody for the worse. Some of the town's families still have hard feelings."

"I'm aware, Freddie. And the old arguments over who owes who what, or who owns what lands should be left alone. I agree."

Freddie continued, "But if that chicken spook is acting up in her pub, I guess she has no choice."

I laughed, "The grumpy chicken does get your attention when she is upset. So Ginger has another mess on her hands. Maybe Lily and I should visit the pub tonight, get the gang together to help her."

Freddie wondered, "Why do Y'all like to work together like that?"

"It's what we do in a small town. We help each other. And Lily and I love the thrill of sleuthing. Sometimes, it even includes motorcycle rides"

Freddie smiled at the image of Edith on a motorbike. "I heard about you on the back of Guardrail's bike that one time. Dog Breath was in here one time, called your group some weird name. Does your group have a name."

I laughed. "Oh, pish posh. Since when do you listen to Dog. We're just a group of friends helping each other."

"OK. I'm not being nosy, just wondering. Let me know if I can help ya with anything else and thanks for the order. It is so hard to make a profit with everyone ordering online these days. I appreciate you coming here."

"I know and I'm glad to give you my business. But I should go now and catch Lily up on the latest news. Bye for now."

I made my way from the general store, jingling the vigilant bell on the door. I sensed pending mayhem and needed to get home quick. The Grumpy Chicken was at the center of another strange mystery. Lily and I would want to partake in the fun.

Chapter Four

Piper

After an early start, Digger and I spied Atlanta's skyline at ten-thirty a.m. and we made a beeline for my former employer, the Atlanta Journal-Constitution. While I currently write news articles for my own paper, The Potter's Mill Oracle, I had new business with my old editor slash boss. After the Ghost Hounds filmed an episode in The Grumpy Chicken, a larger market for many of my written pieces emerged and contacts at the Atlanta newspaper helped syndicate my stories of the strange events in the pub. The series developed a growing audience, plus recent pub events suggested future narratives were forthcoming. We had plenty to discuss.

Digger shifted his seat belt and twisted to get comfortable. "Why do you go back to an old workplace so much?"

"Well, I still have friends there and we keep in touch.

And we do some business together. It's good for both of us."

Digger shook his head. "I don't get big city life. When you quit a job in my book, it's includes leaving and not going back to do business with them. But oh well."

"When we get there, you want to come in, see the press rooms and printing presses?"

"Sure. Only seen that in a movie."

Atlanta was my home for a number of years. After my parents divorced, my Mom left Potter's Mill but still tried to domineer my life and Dad was a mess, so I decided to move to the big city and work for a real newspaper. It was an exciting time working at the paper and I made a ton of friends. But after a while, newsroom politics and big city life grew stale. Then I started to have an odd compulsion to play Keno and ran up some debt. After six years in the city, I also started to miss my childhood friends, so it was time for me to move back to small-town life, a simpler existence. However, every other month, at times more, I journey back to the metropolis to visit acquaintances and explore some of my favorite spots. This is a compromise that satisfies my need for the culture and energy of a major city without turning my back on my real home, Potter's Mill. And I don't have a chance to play Keno and get into more trouble.

As it turns out, Digger provided better company on the three-hour drive than anticipated. I asked, "Digger, what are you going to do after we're done at the newspaper, while I go to lunch with Jayson?"

"I don't know. I'll find something to do."

"You want me to drop you off someplace?"

He shrugged. "Where would you drop me?"

"You want to see the World of Coca-Cola?"

"Why would I spend a couple of hours looking at bottles of soda?"

"It's a lot more than Coke bottles."

"No thanks."

"Well, what are you interested in?"

"I don't know. Pick-up trucks, beer, football, tools."

"There's a college football hall of fame."

"Nah, too close to a museum. I don't do museums."

I sighed. "Well, I know a real interesting hardware store in a walking mall. It's in Buckhead. It's more of a step back in time than it is a store."

"That sounds good."

"So we have a plan. That will work well. We're to meet with the historical society at two-thirty and that is also in Buckhead. All our business is to the north of midtown and that makes it easier. We should have plenty of time unless traffic is bad. Which it is most of the time. But we have all day and there is no rush."

"When you go to lunch, don't get caught up in the moment with your old fling and lose track of the time. I know how it is when two young-ins get all googly-eyed with each other."

I laughed, "O…M…G. There is so much wrong with that statement. Jayson and I are just friends and I want to get to the historical society, too. Don't worry."

We arrived at the paper and conducted our business as planned. It went quick, including Digger's tour. We left and on the way to the car, I spotted it. "Digger, where in the world did you get ink on you?"

"What?"

"You have ink on your overalls."

"Well, look at that."

"You're not getting ink on my seats. Wait." I dug into the trunk and found an old blanket. "Here sit on this."

"OK. You sure? Looks like a nice blanket."

"It's fine. It's an old beach blanket."

Digger placed the blanket on the seat, making sure it was secure and would prevent ink from soiling my car. I underestimated my fellow investigator. He was considerate and careful.

We buckled up and headed for our lunchtime

appointments. I dropped Digger at Buckhead Atlanta and went to meet Jayson. To my surprise, my old boyfriend found a new girlfriend. And that was all he wanted to talk about, so I cut the lunch short.

On returning to the walking mall, I found Digger chatting with a crowd of people. The old gravedigger engaged the audience and I caught him in a rare smile. "Digger, what are you doing?"

"Emily here recognized me from The Ghost Hounds episode and had some questions. Seems a few more people had questions, too."

I failed to prevent my jaw from hanging. The man who sat at the bar quietly, enduring all kinds of bad cemetery jokes, now entertained a crowd. I stammered, "Well…well, let's go. We have an appointment to keep."

Digger turned to the crowd and waved. "Thanks to all. And thanks, Emily, for the soda. That was real nice of you. I have to go now. We have another riddle to investigate."

We climbed into the car and I asked, "Did she really get you that soda?"

"Yep. Said it was thanks for taking the time to chat. And she asked for an autograph. It was my first."

"I don't believe this. You're worried about me getting all googly-eyed, but you're out losing your autograph virginity."

"It just sounds weird when you put it that way." Digger eyed me sideways.

I sighed, "Let's just get to the Atlanta History Center. This lunch period did not go as envisioned."

Once again, we buckled up and made a short drive. We arrived to find the history center was a huge complex. Our appointment was with a respected historian I worked with back in my days as a journalist in Atalanta, but first, we had to find him.

We parked in the large municipal parking lot and walked, for maybe a mile. Old farms, residences, and botanical gardens passed by as we hunted for the research center. After checking the map app on my phone a few times, the modern, masonry building was in front of us and it contrasted with all the surrounding historic places.

Digger struggled to catch his breath. "This place is huge. I hope he has comfortable chairs in there. I need to sit."

I chuckled, "Well, there's only one way to find out. Let's go see him."

We made our way to the front door and let ourselves into a large, unattended lobby. I spotted a directory next to a phone, found his name, and dialed the number next to it. He answered and said he was on his way to the foyer.

After a minute, Blake Winston came into the glass-walled entry to find us waiting. He had a full head of bushy gray hair and was in his mid-sixties, but still full of energy. He wore beige khakis and a green button down shirt, topped with a lab coat. His eyes sparkled as he examined both of us, revealing how this man's mind constantly analyzed and contemplated everything. "Piper Freeman, welcome! We have much to discuss. I did some research earlier, based on what you told me and the photos you sent. Now I am now dying to examine this locket in person."

I smiled at him. "Hello to you, too. This is quite the place."

"That's right, you've never been here. When we did prior business I met with you at the Constitution's offices, or at some coffee shop."

"We did like our coffee shop meetings."

Blake turned to Digger. "I am Blake Winston, pleased to meet you." He nodded to the gravedigger, studying the man.

"Hello to you, too." Digger took a small step back.

Blake continued, "I see you visited the printing presses at the Constitution."

Digger wrinkled his nose. "How do ya know that."

"Ink on your pants."

I interjected. "Blake doesn't miss a thing. It's why I asked him to help with the locket."

Blake subtly bowed to me and said, "Thank you. Well, come on in. I'll give you a quick tour. This is a private research center, not open to the public, so you're getting a behind the scenes tour."

Digger huffed. "Great. This looks like a museum, this should be loads of fun." I shot a stern look in reply. He must have received the message, because he countered, "I'll be good."

To Digger's delight, Professor Winston rushed our tour and in minutes, we arrived at his research laboratory. He wanted to examine the locket, not be a tour guide, that was clear.

The room was filled with shelves loaded with boxes of old stuff. In the center, two large tables held an elaborate microscope and computers. One a number of rolling carts, bins held specimens and various paperwork. Blake pointed to wooden armchairs in front of the microscope and we sat.

Digger exclaimed, "Oh my goodness, that feels good. I work on my feet all day, but the walking around this place was brutal."

I smacked his arm. "We're here on business. Focus."

Blake said, "Yes, business. I researched the Byrne family name and they are a key family in the history of Potter's Mill. Many of the current local families have ties back to them, though some are hard to track due to poor record keeping."

I pointed out, "That's interesting, so why isn't the Byrne name known in town?"

"Well, that is part of what is interesting about them. A man named Conner Walsh helped develop the pottery mill into a thriving business. He also helped the local farming community become one of the biggest suppliers of sweet onions. Potter's Mill was a hub of business back then Conner Walsh had his hand in much of it."

Digger fidgeted and complained. "What are we talking about this old guy for? What has it got to do with the locket?"

Blake replied with a calm voice. "I'm getting to that. See Conner married Erin Byrne. And they had five children. Conner and Erin's sons both died in the Civil War. So the three daughter's went on to marry but the Walsh name ended after one new generation. It's why the Walsh's are not well known today in Potter's Mill. But their blood flows through many of the locals there. That is profound."

Digger threw his hands in the air. "My head is going to explode. We asked you about an Erin Byrnes, but you keep talking about this Walsh dude."

"Digger, that is what they call you right?" We both nodded yes and Blake continued, "See, Erin Byrnes married Conner Walsh. Her parents moved to Potter's Mill and they were the only Byrnes in town. She was an only child so the Byrnes name ended with her marriage. Erin Byrnes' name became Erin Walsh."

I asked, "You seem real excited about finding she was married to Conner. Why?"

"You don't understand. Erin Walsh is almost famous in some circles. And many of the stories are, well let's say, inflated tall tales. However, a piece from her past falls into our laps giving us a chance to examine it. I hope that the locket will decipher a little about what is true and what is false in the myths and legends that surround her."

Digger snorted. "Well, what are some of these old legends about her. I never heard any of 'em."

Blake inhaled. "One of the most repeated myths states she was cursed, forced to haunt Potter's Mill for eternity."

I gasped. "And her locket is found on a headstone in the Potter's Mill cemetery. I am starting to understand why you are interested in this locket."

Blake's eyes sparkled. "Can I see it?"

Digger glared back at Blake and said, "No!"

Chapter Five

Ida

As we exited, the bell over the general store's door jingled. The Angel's Glow story Edith told us was interesting, but was of no help with our search for information on the mystery woman. I wished to be back in my office, with all my computers, where I was most comfortable.

My mom died giving birth to me, so Dad raised me alone. He told me as a little girl to pursue whatever I wanted and he supported all my wild experiments, including the karate phase. The arrival of computers in our homes enthralled me and Dad made sure I had the latest and greatest machine. Because of him, I found my calling. And right now, my instincts told me that I should be using my skills to find information on Erin Byrnes, but I was squandering time with this tour of town. However, I do trust Ginger. She has good instincts and is an excellent detective. This current task required patience and I attempted to conform.

At least it was a nice sunny day, perfect for a walk, and many of the shopkeepers on Main Street were out setting up sidewalk displays or chatting with the passersby. We started for town hall and marched on for one whole half block before we halted. Bessie Houston worked in front of her store stacking something colorful when she spotted us and yelled, "Ginger, a minute if you could?"

Ginger waved and nodded yes, so we diverted over to Sew Fabric to chat. Ginger asked, "What can I do for ya?"

"It's been so hectic in the pub with things like the television show, the attempt on your ex-husband's life, and all the tourists that come and go to see The Grumpy Chicken. But things have calmed a little and I thought we could have a crafts night again at the pub." Bessie waved at the storefront to emphasize the knitting and crafts.

Ginger glanced up at the sky, then back at Bessie. "Sure, that's a great idea. We haven't had Stitch 'N Bitch in a long while. It's time and we have lots to gossip about."

Bessie made a face like she bit down on a dozen lemons. "No, I hate that name. Please don't say that. It sounds so crude. But I would like to host a crafts night and we can do something special with the food."

Bones added, "No chicken wings. They're bad luck."

"Bones. That's just silly. We can make whatever you

like. Bessie." Ginger glared at Bones with a smile. She had a way of telling people things with her eyes. Bones understood, be accommodating with the customer wishes even when you are right and they are wrong.

"Oh, I haven't thought about what to serve. I have to talk to Carl. He looks forward to your food more than me, so he's the one to pick."

Ginger smiled. "Whatever you want. Hey, have you ever heard of a woman named Erin Byrnes?"

Bessie jiggled her head no. "Not really. Why do you ask?"

I said, "Digger found a mysterious locket and the grumpy chicken didn't like it. To be honest the feathered poltergeist threw a fit. So we are trying to learn more about it and this woman's name was inscribed on the back of the locket. Freddie thought the Byrnes name was part of the town's history."

Bessie's eyes grew wide. "Wow. There is always something going on with you guys, isn't there. That is intriguing. Ya know, I have an old trunk in my attic with all kinds of old stuff. Most of it is about Potter's Mill. Maybe something in the chest can help you find this Erin Byrnes?"

Ginger glanced at Bones and me. We both nodded to confirm and she said, "Bessie, that is real nice of you. We won't take too much of your time, but that would be great."

"Sure, let me tell Carl I'm heading to the house for a few minutes." Bessie went into the store for a few minutes then came back carrying her handbag.

We walked a short way to their old, but quaint home surrounded by the cliche white picket fence. "Come on in, the place is a mess, but the attic is worse. It's so dusty." Bessie opened the door and a black Labrador met us, tail wagging. She patted the friendly dog and said, "Hello, Macrame, how's my good girl?"

The building was an old farmhouse, three stories tall. We climbed all the stairs with dog in tow, and to our dismay, Bessie pulled another folding set of steps from the ceiling. Out of breath, everyone climbed the last narrow steps into the dark, musty attic, except for the pooch.

Bessie pulled a string and light filled the small space. All kinds of junk surrounded us like boxes, clothing, old lamps, and broken chairs. Under a stack of discarded clothing, some still holding idle hangers in the neck hole, sat an ancient wooden trunk. Bessie pointed to it and said, "That's it. Carl's father left it to him and it's filled with all kinds of weird books and documents. Most of it is Potter's Mill history."

Bones moved the clothes pile and tried to open the chest. Bessie chuckled, "You need this." She held up an old skeleton key.

Bones took the key and unlocked the trunk. A gray cloud formed and we all placed a hand over our mouths to filter the air we breathed. After allowing a minute to literally let the dust settle, we peered into the chest. Bessie was right, this old-fashioned trunk held lots of stuff.

Bones gushed. "Holy moly, look at all this. This book is about farming in Bear's Paw Swamp. And this one is a catalog for the pottery that used to be made at the mill."

I leafed through the items and discovered old pottery catalogs and ledgers to account for the produce grown on nearby farms. Trivia, mostly useless, but I was learning a thing or two. For instance, back in eighteen-fifty, I confirmed farming and pottery were the two businesses that supported and grew the town. After a few minutes of scanning items in the trunk, it appeared. An old piece of parchment clung to the backboards of the trunk, as if trying to stay out of sight. I carefully removed it and unfolded the document. It was a map.

Bones gasped. "Wow. That's so cool. It looks like it's the town back a thousand years ago."

Ginger laughed. "That's too long Bones. This town is only about two hundred years old."

I studied the map. "It says here eighteen fifty-eight. So, yeah, Ginger is right. It's the town one hundred and sixty years ago."

Ginger examined the map. "Hey, look at this. The pub is on the map. But it was called The Fickle Waterwheel."

I saw some small print under the pub name. "It says the pub was owned by the Walsh family."

Bones muttered, "Who's the Walsh family?"

Ginger looked at me. "Ida, can you help answer that?"

I pulled out my phone. "Sure, let's consult the web." I punched in the search and found thousands of Walsh's. "I need to spend more time on this. That is a common name and I need to refine the search." I tried focusing on Potter's Mill in the nineteenth century and that helped. "There does seem to be a family that worked and lived in town back then, but nothing about them on the net that says they ran a farm or pub." I scanned the search results. "But get this, there was an Erin Walsh. And there are lots of references to odd occurrences associated with her…But they seem as reliable as Bigfoot sightings."

The dust took a victim. Ginger began coughing and descended the attic stairs. She hollered back at us, "This dust is killing me. And there's really only room for two to work. Bring down anything of interest for us to make copies down at town hall. Bessie and I will wait downstairs. We have business to discuss anyway, for the next crafts night." Bessie and Ginger backed out of the tight attic space and down the stairs.

Bones hollered after them, "Will do." He looked at me and whispered, "She trusts us to do this?"

"Sure, why not?"

Bones dove back into the chest. "Well, let's get to it."

We rummaged all the old catalogs and ledgers. The Byrnes name did not appear, but the name The Fickle Waterwheel and Walsh appeared in a number of places. The old documents told us the family participated in the pottery and farming business of the time, but nothing more.

"Bones, I'm not sure, but I think the map is important. We should take it to make a copy."

"Not any of the books?"

"No. They tell us who traded onions and pottery here, sure. But that's it. Nothing about where they came from, how they died, if they fought in the war, or how they lived. We can come back for the books if we have to, but I want a copy of the map to better study it."

"What makes the map special?"

"I'm not sure. Here look at this." I handed my phone to Bones after pulling up a picture of the locket front. "See the engraved pattern?"

"Yeah."

"Now look at the map."

Bones complied and his reaction reminded me of the Grinch story. Instead of his heart growing three sizes, though, his eyeballs grew three sizes to golf balls and they may have even glowed in the bad lighting. He uttered, "It's the same scrolly things around the pub name."

"My eyes are not what they used to be. But I thought so, too. I want to check it out under better lighting and see if there is any other information on the map. I can do a better internet search back in the hack shack, too."

Bones added, "Let me look at the books again. We might have missed something." And he did. The young grill master and dishwasher went through every book and ledger a second time. After twenty minutes, he sighed, "Well, that wasn't real productive. But this one book has one transaction that is different from all the others."

I smiled, "It was good that you rechecked. And it gave me time to sift through some on the Walsh's I found in my queries. Seems there was a Walsh that married a girl from the Byrne family. An Erin."

Bones gasped. "So you found our Erin Byrne."

"Maybe. I got some more deep web searches going on back at the hack shack. I will see what they find and will wait till then to make any conclusions."

"So the map goes with us. And I want to take this book, too. The quantities of goods traded is large for one deal and maybe it means something." Bones displayed the book to me.

"Well, that sounds like a good find. Good job. You may have just earned your grumpy chicken detective badge."

Bones popped, "You mean we even have a cool secret name and titles?"

"No, you nitwit. I was just saying you did good. Why does everyone think we need a name? Jeez."

"I'm sorry. I just wanted to be part of the gang."

"Now you're getting it, we're just a group of friends who help each other. Now let's go show Ginger what we found."

We put everything away, headed down the attic stairs, and folded the narrow contraption back into the ceiling. After making a pit stop in the upstairs guest room to clean up, we headed down to the first floor. Bessie and Ginger sat in plush wing chairs sipping tea in the living room. Macrame lied sleeping at Bessie's feet. Ginger spotted us first. "Well, the dust miners return!" The dog woke and came over to check us out, tail again wagging.

I patted the canine and glanced at Ginger. "Some of us are apparently tougher than others."

She chuckled in response. "I'll give you this one, Ida. But I was doing nothing anyway, the space was too small."

"Well, Bones and I found a couple of things that are interesting. Is it OK, Bessie, if we take them to make copies?" I held up the map and Bones displayed the book for her to see.

Bessie nodded. "Sure. I want to help."

Ginger added, "So are we ready to head over to town hall?"

I nodded. "Sure."

Ginger put her cup of tea on the coffee table. "Bessie, this was real sweet of you. Thank you. And I look forward to our next Stitch…I mean craft night."

Bessie bowed her head to indicate thank you and she smiled. "I can't wait for it. I will let you know what Carl picks for the menu."

Ginger smiled and nodded back at her, then we all made for the door. Once outside, Ginger asked, "So, Ida, was that worth the time?"

I answered, "Sure, if nothing else it gave me time to look at some my internet searches and they are finding information. I found an Erin Byrnes, but that is her maiden name, and her married name my be Erin Walsh. If this Erin Walsh is our Erin Byrnes, well, there's lots of weird tales on the internet about her as Erin Walsh. We should get to the bottom of who Erin Byrnes is today. And maybe more."

"Why maybe more?"

"I don't know. The map just feels like it's important to me."

Bones blurted out, "Tell Ginger about the scroll work."

I chuckled, "It may be nothing, but the scrolls around The Fickle Waterwheel pub name on the map are the same as the scrolls on the front of the locket."

"Wow. No, that sounds like something. How did I miss that?" Ginger tilted her head like she was searching for an answer to her own question. "I couldn't see a thing up there. That dust cloud refused to settle."

"I agree. We need to look at the map in a better light. And Bones found an unusual transaction in one of the ledgers." I pointed at the book he held.

Bones added, "Yeah. Seems an awful lot of goods were traded in one day. So, I took that book, too."

Ginger said, "Well, every clue is important. Great, on to town hall."

We walked with a new spring our step and a focused sense of purpose. That lasted for a whole minute till Beth Givens appeared on the sidewalk and destroyed it all.

Chapter Six

Digger

Blake Winston grated my nerves and this meeting frustrated me because I took a vacation day to make this trip. He blathered on with nothing useful, this was wasting our time. I grew up on a farm and worked hard every day, and sometimes at night helping to make moonshine. My parents taught me it was simple; if you slacked off, you went hungry. You made sure to use every single available hour to do something productive. Back at the cemetery, lawns needed grooming and the old perimeter wrought iron fence needed repair. The place could do without me for a day, but what was I doing sitting here listening to this fool? It was time to leave.

We asked him to help with a few simple questions and he was telling tall tales about a stranger. And he constantly looked at me like he wanted to pick my pockets or read my mind. I hated it so I said what was on my mind. "I found this locket and I will pick who I show it to. I think it's time for us to go."

Blake looked at me like I farted at his wedding. He said, "I'm sorry. I don't mean to offend. I'm just curious and always want to know more about the people I come in contact with. Where do they come from, who were their ancestors, what do they do for a living – it's just habit. When I was younger, I did make a number of people uncomfortable with my need to study everyone, but I learned to be more polite and discrete about it. You are most perceptive and I apologize."

Piper glanced at me, her face red. "Digger, it's alright. Blake is just excited about your find and he can help us. Let him have a look."

"Piper, I'm sorry. But I've never experienced anything like I did when I took this locket out of my pocket in the pub. It got cold all on its own and I could tell it's important. Like it was able to make me feel what it wanted."

Blake squinted at me. "So is it telling you something now?"

"Kind of. It doesn't want to leave my possession."

Blake made a long face. "This is fascinating. But I don't fully understand what is happening." He paused. "Alright then, the locket isn't to leave your possession. You are going to just let me examine it. You can sit right next to me and it never leaves your control."

I turned to Piper, searching for her opinion. She looked

at me like a big sister telling me it was alright to eat my spinach. I snapped back at her. "Don't look at me like I'm a ten-year-old. I get your point. I'm being too protective."

Piper added, "Overprotective? You're acting like Gollum with the one ring to rule them all. Holy cow!"

"Who is Gollum?"

Piper laughed. "I should have guessed you don't know who Gollum is, 'Lord of the Rings' doesn't have pick-up trucks or football."

Blake interrupted, "I don't mean to be rude, but we only have so much time. Digger, if you would be so good as to place the locket on this little platform right here. Under the microscope."

I sensed Piper trusted this man and he was trying meet half way by letting me place the locket. "Alright." The flap on my pocket was fastened tight to make sure the locket was safe. After wrestling with the button, I reached in and retrieved it.

Blake pointed, "Right there, that will be fine."

I put it down and Blake turned on a special light. It was like a goose neck that he bent in all kinds of directions till it shot centered bright light down on the locket. He then focused the microscope. I was surprised when the image popped on a computer monitor. Apparently, you do not have look into the microscope eyepieces in today's modern world. You can watch on

TV.

Blake pointed. "Just as I thought. See that."

Piper and I squinted at the enlarged image of the locket back. Fancy scrolls and decoration surrounded the engraved "To my love Erin Byrnes." But under magnification, we saw initials. Someone secretly engraved tiny letters inside one of the decorative decorations on back.

Blake added, "H.C. This was custom made by Henri Chorette. He was a French jewelry maker that came to New York City. He opened shop and his pieces sold well to the wealthy from eighteen-twenty to eighteen-forty. Wearing his jewelry was a sign of wealth just before the civil war."

I had to point out, "There ya go again. Talking about some dead guy we don't know or care about."

Blake smiled at me. "Be patient. It's a clue where this came from. Henri's shop was in New York. Conner Walsh had this made special for Erin Byrnes as a sign of his love. It may have even been an engagement gift. So, Conner had money back then and traveled. He would need to actually travel to New York to get this locket back then. There was no Amazon in the nineteenth century."

I huffed. "So the guy had money and traveled."

Blake sat up straight. "Well, the records show he played a key role in developing Bear's Paw Swamp into

Potter's Mill."

I rolled my eyes this time and interrupted. "Someone shoot me! This is so boring! Wait a minute. Did you say Bear's Paw Swamp?" Blake nodded yes. I added, "That's the name of the swamp down near the cemetery."

Blake's face lit up. "Yes it is. But back before the Civil War, the whole area was called Bear's Paw Swamp. It earned the name from a legend that a hunter found huge bear prints in the swamp. He attempted for years to trap the huge black bear, but failed. The bear paw prints were said to be almost as large as Babe the Blue Ox."

Piper said, "Digger is right, that's all interesting, but we don't care about Paul Bunyan's pet. What about Erin Byrnes?"

Blake continued, "Sorry, so Conner Walsh owned a large farm in Bear Paw's Swamp and opened a number of businesses in the burgeoning town. He had five children and they owned and operated some of them, like the general store and the local pub."

Piper interrupted, "The Grumpy Chicken?"

Blake shook his head. "No. It was called The Fickle Waterwheel back then. I haven't confirmed if it is the same or a different pub yet. They're both in the same spot, but so many buildings were destroyed during the war. I assume the old pub was burned during Sherman's March, almost all buildings there were destroyed."

I sighed, "So where is this all going?"

Blake smiled back at me. "The pub is haunted by a grumpy chicken right?"

I glared at the odd man. "We didn't need to come to Atlanta to find that out. Me and Piper have seen the grumper do things with our own eyes."

Blake continued, "Follow me. You have a chicken ghost. And Conner's children, well more important Erin's children, ran the old pub."

I slumped in my chair. "I give up. I don't know where this is going."

Piper hissed at me, "Hush!"

"See there is an old legend about General Lee. And it involves a chicken." Blake used his hands to animated his sentence as he spoke.

I stood, "I'm done. Babe the Blue Ax, or ox or whatever, rich guys in the Civil War, a legend in the swamp, now General Lee and his chicken; this guy is all over the place, Piper. We're wasting our time."

Blake waved at me to sit and continued, "They're all connected. During and after the Civil War, ghost stories were rampant. And many of them remain unexplained today. There was one in particular about General Lee that always interested me. It may be the key to your mystery. See, a Virginia farmer gave a flock of chickens to the general and his troops ate them all, except one. This particular chicken survived by making her nest over General Lee's tent. Lee took a liking to the little black chicken and even gave it a name, Nellie. Every day, Lee raised the flap of his tent and she used the tent as a roost. Nellie even started to lay eggs under the general's cot everyday. But just before the Battle of the Wilderness, Lee's personal cook was out of food and had no choice but to slaughter and serve Nellie to all the generals. Lee was furious and it was said it was the only time he reprimanded his slave."

I shrugged, "So?"

Blake's eyes were alive. "What if the chicken was mad, just like General Lee. It's possible that this chicken haunting your pub is General Lee's Nellie."

Piper moaned. "I don't know. Digger might be right. What's this all got to do with the locket?"

Blake took a deep breath. "Well, if Conner Walsh, Erin's husband, had money he certainly had acquaintances before and during the war. It would almost be impossible for a prominent man in a growing town to stay neutral. And this locket proves Conner traveled, he would have to go to New York to buy this locket. It is possible he knew Lee from his travels and somehow the ghost of Lee's pet chicken, Nellie, ended up haunting the pub in Bear Paw's Swamp."

I laughed but Piper frowned. She said, "There are a lot of missing pieces if that is true. How did the chicken get to Georgia, and Potter's Mill in particular? That's a big question."

"Yes it is, but this is where Erin Walsh comes in. She was considered mad by some, but others thought she was brilliant, even clairvoyant. The stories of bizarre and mysterious events involving her are many. It is possible that Nellie's ghost and Erin Walsh had a connection."

I groaned. "Again, this is weak." Piper glared at me and I held my tongue from further remarks.

Blake shrugged, "Maybe. But what do you know about the lost confederate gold?"

I stared at the babbling fool. "Now you want us to go on a treasure hunt?"

"No, but there was millions in gold unaccounted for after the war. And Conner Walsh had money. What if the gold was hidden in Potter's Mill during the war? It would account for a small town popping up in the middle of nowhere and confederates would have been in and out of town to stash the gold. Maybe even Lee himself. So if the gold was hidden there, maybe the chicken is associated with it somehow. And if Erin was clairvoyant, she could communicate with the chicken."

Piper made a noise. "Hmmm. Star does seem to be able to communicate with the grumpy chicken."

Blake popped, "Oh Star, I remember her from TV in the episode about the pub on The Ghost Hunters. She is so pretty. And a medium, right?"

I plopped my head back on my shoulders and stared at

the ceiling. "Yeah, but Star has nothing to do with why we're here. So what on earth are you trying to say?"

Blake paused for dramatic effect. "There may be millions in gold stashed in Potter's Mill and the ghost of Lee's pet chicken is guarding it. Bear's Paw Swamp was remote, and back then, there was a potential medium in town who would be able to communicate with the chicken spirit, to work with it. It was a perfect place to safely stash the gold. It all fits, albeit a few pieces of evidence to prove it are missing. But after the town was razed by Sherman, nothing was left, including Erin. She died that day trying to save some horses from a burning barn. The gold's secrets would have been lost with no way to communicate with the chicken. But now her locket appears and finds it's way to the pub. It's a sign, a message, and it could be Erin herself trying to talk to us."

I felt a flash in my stomach. "Star said the grumpy chicken was worried. It could have been upset that gold was in danger of being found?"

Blake leaned towards Piper and me. "Precisely."

Piper gasped. "I'm starting to understand why you are so excited."

Chapter Seven

Ginger

Tea with Bessie was enjoyable and perhaps helpful. As we made our way down the sidewalk for town hall, the sun shone and the temperature moderated, a beautiful day for a walk. However, Beth Givens was a rain cloud heading straight at us. I contemplated what tales she was busy spinning with her gossip and decided it was best to talk with her for a minute. She met us on the sidewalk in front of the sandwich shop, short of our intended destination. "Hello Ginger, looks like you three are up to no good. I heard the chicken ghost made a ruckus yesterday. I assume you are out and about today because of it, looking for something."

I sighed, "You are correct. We're looking for information about an Erin Byrnes. We want to know more about her." No need to say more than necessary.

Beth looked down and shook her head no. "Not a name I know. Was she one of the pesky tourist who come to your squalid little pub? When and why was she here?"

Bones chuckled. "No, she was here before any of us were, back during the Civil War, maybe. We think she lived here."

Beth's lips puckered. "Oh, the war. Lots of history there. So many people passed through here then."

I asked, "What does that mean?"

Beth smiled like she swallowed all the canaries in the south. "But surely you must know. Before and during the war, the underground railroad ran through here and many escaped slaves traveled through Potter's Mill. There were a number of routes to the north, but Savannah was a well known departure point back then. If you were an escaped slave, you headed for the coastal port to find passage by ship to New England."

Ida cracked, "Every town in the south dealt with fleeing slaves, so that is true of all towns back then."

Beth answered, "No, the road through here was a main route to Savannah and that meant a path to a free life for many slaves. However, this was a well known fact to both the escaped slaves and the confederates. So it was also perilous. The soldiers hunted the escapees and many of the runners were killed as they scurried for freedom."

Bones interrupted her, "That's awful, how many?"

Beth's face showed fake sadness. "Thousands. There were over six-hundred thousand soldiers who died in the great war. And who knows how many innocents. Record keeping back then was not very good."

Ida pointed at town hall. "Are there any records that may help us in the public archives?"

Beth nodded. "Possibly. The town records that didn't burn during the war are kept there now. Abbey may know better."

Bones shuddered. "I hope she is willing to help. I know she's still mad at me."

Beth laughed, "She is, I'm sure. Being the local playboy is always going to get you into trouble in a small town. I hope you learned your lesson, young man." She looked over her nose at him, then continued, "But she is proud of her work and I expect she will help if she can."

I tried to rescue my youthful employee from shame. "Thank you Beth. But we really have to go in and see Abbey."

Beth waved her hand like a traffic cop signaling stop. "But, Ginger, I didn't get to why I stopped you."

I gave in and played her game. "I'm sorry, so why did you stop us?"

"To talk to your about your supposed chicken ghost. I heard that your spirit is upset and you're looking to know more about it. Is that right?"

"Yes."

"Well, I have long thought the ghost is that of a dead slave or solider from the Civil War. It makes sense. Like I told you, so many passed through here and many were horribly killed. They would have good reason to want to haunt the area. And just now I find out you are looking for a woman from the war era. It all makes sense."

Ida shot back, "Why haunt the pub then? It was built after the war."

Beth shrugged. "It's one of the places where lots of people spend time."

I noted, "Ida is right, the pub was built after the war. So lots of people go to the pub, that might make some sense, but why not haunt one of the old farmhouses around here, or the old mill, or even the old church?"

Beth grinned. "We all know spirits are seen at the old church, so maybe it was occupied by some other poltergeist when your chicken was looking for a place to stay."

Bones was looking at his shoes, rubbing his chin. He picked his head up and said, "There's something I don't get. The spirit seen at the church is usually a woman. But our spirit is a chicken. Not a slave or soldier."

Beth took a quick breath. "That's what makes me think it's a former slave. See, many of the slaves practiced voodoo and magic. And chickens are central in many ways to the occult. We all know chicken's feet are often used in Voodoo, sometimes as talismans."

Bones pinched his eyebrows. "What's a talisman?"

Ida smacked his arm. "You know. A good luck charm or something used for protection from evil or the supernatural."

Bones smacked her arm back. "I didn't know that, thank you miss smarty pants."

I scolded, "Really? Ida, Bones, can we please stay on topic?"

Beth snorted. "So childish. Thank you, Ginger. See, a chicken makes sense and the pub was built just after the war. So it was new and available for those who died during the war to haunt."

It hit me as she spoke, so I asked, "Were the slave's ankles bound?"

Beth tilted her head slightly. "Hmmm. That's a good question. In many cases, I believe so."

"I saw the chicken not too long ago. It limped and I saw why. It had a shackle on its left leg."

Beth's eyes grew wide. "What kind of shackle? Like a wide black band?"

"Yeah. And a few links of a heavy chain dragging from it."

"That's very interesting. I believe that is what was commonly used back then in Georgia. It all fits, the grumpy chicken is a former slave killed while trying to escape. And she haunts us now in return."

Ida shook her head no. "Why can't Star tell that then? She seems to know a lot about the old chicken but never said she was a slave or confederate soldier."

I spun to Ida. "That's a good point. Remind me to visit with Star and ask her."

Beth's face went long. "Ginger, you don't believe me?"

Bones blurted out, "I do, it makes sense."

I glared at Bones and he understood now was not a good time to speak, then I returned my gaze to Beth. "I didn't mean to imply anything. I'm just trying to figure this thing out. And I want to check every resource I can. You bring up some good points. Thank you. But what is the connection to Erin Byrnes? It's a good Irish name that doesn't seem to connect to your theory."

Beth shrugged. "I don't know, but a few Irish families did settle here. So to run across an Irish name is not uncommon. Maybe it was Erin that killed the slave."

Ida asked, "How do we find something like that out?"

Beth snuffled. "What? Am I supposed to know everything. I have no idea. Your the alleged town detectives. You'll have to find that out on your own."

I hated to admit it, but I agreed with Beth for once. The shackle on the grumpy chicken made some sense, but how could I find who she was, how she died? Was it even really a she? We just assumed because it was a chicken and not a rooster. "Well, we should go see Abbey in town hall. I am very interested to see if the archives have anything that can help us."

Beth snickered. "There are plenty of records from the war stowed away in the archives. But if you want ancestry data, why not use some of that fancy DNA testing?"

I chuckled, "That's a bit much for now. We would have to test everyone in town. But an interesting idea." I could tell Beth wanted to talk more, but we needed to somehow break away from her and get on with our day.

Blanche Diaz, one of the co-owners of Potter's Mill recently established art gallery, saved the day. She spotted us and came over. "Ginger, so nice to see you. I was going to swing by the pub later, but this saves me a trip. I found a painting you might be interested in seeing. It's so bizarre but interesting. A patron brought it in for us to clean-up and re-frame. I can't do it justice trying to describe it, you just need to see it. I think you'll be intrigued."

Beth bubbled. "Oh, I would love to see it too."

Blanche prattled back, "Come on by, have a look. We have some nice blackberry wine for our customers. But we can sneak a little."

I took the opportunity to escape Beth Givens' tedium. "Thanks, ladies. We need to keep moving. And Blanche, we'll swing by the art gallery after we stop in town hall for some research. Bye for now." I turned to see Ida and Bones way ahead of me. They were ten yards in front making a beeline to the town hall entrance.

I caught up to them. Ida said, "Those two are made for each other. All that talk about who did this, or did you know that. All gossip, all the time. And who drinks blackberry wine anymore?"

I laughed, "You said it better than I could've. Thank goodness we are getting on with our day."

We entered the town hall and made our way to Abbey, the clerk. She saw us coming and drooped her head. She took a deep breath and raised her eyes to stare at Bones. "Didn't expect to see you here. I see you brought friends and I assume they're not here for your protection, so you must be here on business."

Bones nodded. "Yeah. I'm still very sorry for what I did to you. I like you a lot and never wanted to hurt you."

Abbey broke a tiny smile. "You're a very sweet man, Bones. But you two timed me, or to be more precise, you two timed the girl you were living with."

Bones studied his toes. "I know. I was stupid and I don't want to bring you anymore trouble, honest. But we had some weird things happen yesterday in the pub and we came across a name, Erin Byrnes. We're trying to find out who she is. I thought there might be something in the town's archives and that can help us. Can we have a look?"

She forced a smile. "Of course."

I jumped in. "Abbey, have you ever heard that name, Erin Byrnes, before?"

"No."

"Is there a book or a log that tracks the families or people who have lived here around the time of the war?"

"Not that I know of." Abbey looked at the rows of shelves filled with books. "But that bookcase right there has the oldest records. The ones that survived the fires during the war." She pointed at a particular old wooden set of shelves.

Bones looked up from his toes. "Thanks. You're kind to help us and it was good to see you again."

"Thanks. Now stop jawing with me and get on with it." Abbey suppress a smile trying to form.

We dove into the books and ledgers. It was time consuming and boring. But after ninety minutes, Ida popped, "Look at this, it is an old letter. It's sent from a soldier named Daniel Walsh to his mother Erin Walsh. He was marching to the battle forming at Gettysburg and feared he would not survive. He told his mother that he did not fear death but if he did die, he wanted to honor the Walsh name *and* the Byrnes military history on his mother's side of the family. That would mean Erin Walsh was Erin Byrnes before she married."

Bones sat up straight. "If the Byrnes family had a history in the military, we might be able to find that information."

I sighed. "Yeah. I think you're right Bones. But not here. Piper and Digger are in Atlanta at the historical society. Maybe we should call them and have them followup on it. I'm guessing the historical society in Atlanta will have better records and maybe they can find something."

Ida chuckled. "I wonder how they are making out? Those two are a weird recon team."

I took out my phone. "Only one way to find out. Let's call them." I dialed.

Chapter Eight

Piper

Blake had a brilliant mind, but he babbled at times and wandered from one topic to another. I concentrated to collect useful data and understood we investigated a mystery deeper than a single locket. The ringtone broke my focus.

I flicked the icon to the right and answered. "Hello?"

"Piper, it's Ginger. We may have found something and maybe you can do some followup research while you are at the historical society."

"That sounds promising. What is it?"

"Erin Byrnes may have been Erin Walsh by marriage. But her family had some sort of decorated military history. I'm hoping you can find out what that might be."

"Well, we found Erin was Erin Walsh too. But how

did you find out about her family history?"

"We didn't, it's why I'm asking you to do some looking for us. But we did find a letter from her son, Daniel, that mentioned he wanted to honor her family's military history."

"Well, let me see what Digger and I can find. And on this end, you're not going to believe it. But we might have found out who the grumpy chicken is and why it's bad-tempered."

"Is the grumper a slave or confederate soldier?"

"Nope, good guess. It's the ghost of General Lee's pet chicken and it may be guarding a stash of gold."

"Wow. That's far more complicated."

"Yeah, but you had to be here to hear the whole thing, the pieces seem to fit. The old locket seems to tell Blake, the historian here, that the giver must have had some money and could travel. Blake thinks the giver was Conner Walsh, Erin's future husband, and the make of the locket implies Conner was connected to the outside world and knew key people. But this is the weird part. Blake knows of odd stories about Erin Walsh, says she was a psychic. And that means she could communicate with the chicken ghost who was protecting the south's secret gold stashed in a small, out-of-the-way town. It was a perfect place to hide a treasure."

"So why did the chicken got upset when we found locket?"

"Because it feared we might find the gold."

"Twenty-four carat chicken feathers! This is not what I expected."

"Yeah. Me neither. And I don't want to speak for Digger, but I think he believes it less than you and me."

"Well, can you take advantage of being there and look into the military history of the Byrnes family? Just to be thorough."

"Sure. Everyone is waiting for me here, and unless there is something else, I should go now."

"Nope, already asked for what I need."

"OK, talk to ya later. See ya." I clicked off.

Digger scowled at me. "You speaking for me? What do I not believe?"

"Blake's story of who Erin and the chicken are."

"Oh! That's alright then. His story sounds like hog wash. It's too far fetched."

I turned to Blake. "My friend back home, Ginger, found that the Byrnes may have a decorated military past. Can you check on that for us?"

Blake's eyes sparkled. "Oh, that's *very* interesting. So there may be a tie back to the confederate army we can prove. That may be how Lee knew of Erin."

Digger eyed the energetic historian. "How can you

check something like that for us?"

Blake shot back, "We ask Betty."

I sat up straight. "Who's that?"

Blake smiled. "The lady who knows everything about military life in the nineteenth century. She works at the Smithsonian."

Digger huffed. "Well that sounds like someone we need to talk to."

Blake pushed off the microscope table and rolled across the floor in his chair over to a desk. He picked up a phone and dialed. After saying hello, he put the call on speaker and we heard a woman's voice. "Can you hear me?"

Blake answered, "Yes, I am here with two visitors, Piper and Digger, looking into a mystery. And the military history of a one Byrnes family may be part of it. What do you know about the Byrnes family in the nineteenth century?"

"Oh, yes. I seem to remember a Daniel Byrnes that served in the early nineteenth century." We heard keyboard keys clacking. "Yes, Daniel Byrnes was a respected colonel and did serve in the Army under Andrew Jackson. He fought in a number of wars including the War of Eighteen-Twelve and the Florida Wars. He received numerous awards and died under mysterious conditions during a battle in the First Seminole War. It appears he may have been on a secret assignment at the time, but that was never confirmed."

Blake sighed. "So, under Andrew Jackson, that is interesting. And didn't Jackson have Irish roots?"

Betty replied, "Yes, he was from a Scottish-Irish family."

Blake nodded. "Thanks Betty. As always, you were extremely helpful." He hung up the phone. "So there you go. Army and Irish ties under Andrew Jackson. Daniel Byrnes fought with one of the greats."

I noted, "Ginger said that Erin's son's name was Daniel. It sounds like he was named after his grandfather."

Blake added, "Well, it was common to name sons after the father or a grandfather back then."

I nodded. "It feels right too. So we know who Erin Byrnes was and who her husband was, but the rest is still all theory." I was thinking out loud. "What do we do next?"

Blake chuckled. "We're not done with the locket. I haven't seen the inside yet."

Digger scowled. "You want me to open it?"

"Of course, yes, if you would be so kind." Blake raised his eyebrows to indicate please.

Digger worked the latch and parted the halves. He carefully set the opened locket back down under the microscope.

Blake reset the lighting and lenses and the enlarged pictures on the inside of the locket displayed on a monitor. "Look at this. It is quite beautiful and very interesting. Look at his coat. He is wearing a pin. Let's see if we can tell what it is." He again worked the optics to zoom in on the object. "I can't really tell, but it might be an Underground Railroad symbol."

Digger squinted at the image. "It looks like a block with squiggly lines to me."

"Well that's true. Let me see if we can get a better look." Blake fiddled with the equipment and an image popped out. "There it is! Beautiful. Members of the railroad used quilts hung on laundry lines to communicate. They used symbol sewn into the quilt to secretly pass messages. This symbol was called Bear's Paw and meant follow the bear tracks to stay out of sight, hidden."

I sighed. "And our town was known as Bear's Paw Swamp. So does this mean Conner Walsh was part of the Underground Railroad? Or does the symbol signify the town's name?"

Blake rubbed his chin. "It could mean both. I assumed the legend of the giant bear paws was how Potter's Mill got it's initial name. But maybe there is more to that story."

Chapter Nine

Bones

We departed town hall victorious. The information in the letter from Erin's son provided a new avenue to explore and we confirmed the identity of Erin Byrnes. The sleuthing business was exciting and I began to understand why Ginger was so passionate about solving mysteries.

But we were not done for the day and now headed to the art gallery. I thought about leaving for the pub's kitchen to start catching up on the mountain of dirty pans waiting for me, but this was too much fun and I wanted to continue my first day of detective work. Plus, I could handle the work load and I wanted to help Ginger. The O'Mallory's gave me a job when I was sixteen and have always helped me. My mom raised me alone after dad left while she was pregnant. And mom was not what you would call the motherly type. In many ways the Ginger and Tom were my family and the pub was my home.

Blanche and her sister Cathy met us as we entered the art gallery. "Ginger, Ida, Bones, so nice to see you. You must be here to take a look at the picture I told you about." Blanche pointed to a big picture on a tripod, covered with a purple satiny cloth.

Ginger said, "We are very curious to see what you found. It sounded interesting."

Blanche smiled. "You can say that. But have a look for yourself." She moved over to the covered painting and pulled the the cloth off of the image.

I gasped. "Holy moly that looks old."

Ida remarked, "It is old. But there is a beauty to it, even though the colors are too dark. Why are old painting so dark and void of color?"

Cathy replied, "That was the style back then. Partly due to the paints that were available. You couldn't get any color you wanted and bright colors were expensive, even if you could find them. And if you used a bright color, the quality was not good and faded out quickly over time."

Ginger added, "That's interesting Cathy, but I'm more interested in what's going on in the painting."

I looked closely. There were four black slaves, some wearing shackles, talking to a Caucasian woman who worked with some old contraption. They appeared to be in a field and there was a barn in the background. But the odd part was the angels circling in the sky.

Blanche said, "The woman is churning butter. And the slaves are asking her for help. At least that is what we think is happening. And the angels indicate something important is happening. The title of the painting is "The Refusal. Cathy and I are still arguing about what that means, but you can see the slave woman are pleading with her, probably for help. So The Refusal makes sense in that context."

Ginger pointed. "So why the angels for that?"

Cathy laughed. "That is what we are still arguing about. Well that and if she is in Potter's Mill."

I studied the painting again. "Hey Ida, look at this. The bucket next the butter churner. It has writing on it. It says The Fickle Waterwheel."

Ida gasped, "Son of churn. You found something there Bones."

Blanche cut in, "We saw that, too, but did not know what The Fickle Waterwheel meant."

Ida smiled. "We do. Look at this." She unfolded the old map with care and showed them the pub name on the old document.

Ginger added, "So it's Potter's Mill, back when it was called Bear's Paw Swamp."

I failed to keep it to myself any longer. "Who are these woman? Is there anyway to tell?"

Blanche looked at me. "Bones, that is the same

question I keep asking. There is emotion in this painting and I keep asking why it was important for someone to paint this moment with these five people. Who are they and why is this important enough to spend the time and money to document it as an image."

Ginger held her phone up. "You mind if I take a couple of pictures of this?"

Blanche shook her head no. "Not at all. Just don't touch the painting. The oils on your fingers will damage it."

Ginger snapped the pictures and Ida followed suit. "No insult, Ginger, but your phone is ancient. I am guessing my phone has better resolution."

Ginger scowled at Ida, "Well excuse me. I'm just a simple pub owner. I don't own all the latest and greatest electronics"

"I know. Like I said, no insult intended. I just want some good pictures for us to analyze if we need them." Ida was actually blushing.

Ginger grinned. "I hate it when you're right at my expense."

I had one more question. "Who brought the painting in to you for work?"

Ida popped back at me. "Hey, Bones, I was going to ask that, too."

Blanche's eyes widened and she sighed. "That's the

weird part. The painting was found by Dorothy Miller in her barn. The Fluffy Pillow has been in her family forever and they saved all the old stuff every time they upgraded the place. Dottie told me an idea was kicking around in her head for a while, but something told her that this was finally the right time to do it. She was looking for old paintings to display in B&B to pay homage to the town's past when she found it. It was in need of work when she found it, so she brought it to us."

Ginger asked, "When was that?"

Cathy looked at the ground. "Hmm, about two days ago."

Ida gasped. "That's the same day as when Digger found the locket."

Blanche asked, 'What locket?"

Ginger replied, "It's a long story. I'll have to tell you later. We need to get over to Star's place. There's a lot to talk to discuss with her."

We excused ourselves and crossed Main Street to make the short walk to Star's New Age Shop. On entering, the big table in the center of the store with the crystal ball was hard to miss. Star came from her office in the back and her long dress flowed in the air as she walked. "Welcome. You brought a crowd. What can I do for you?"

Ginger said, "We unearthed some information today and now we have a few questions for you, if you have a minute."

Star motioned to the table. "Sure. Let's take a seat."

As we sat Ginger asked, "You've received messages from the grumpy chicken before. Can you tell if it is a man or a woman? Or a slave or a confederate soldier?"

Star smiled. "Sometimes I get those kind of details. But your chicken is odd. Very angry sometimes, and other times I sense she is very humble. But I am sure it is a she. Whether she is a slave or soldier, I don't know."

"Did woman fight in the Civil War?" The questions just kept popping out of me today.

Star looked at me with her pretty eyes. "I'm not sure, Bones, but I don't think so. Why?"

I may have blushed but tried to act casual. "Everything today points to the Civil War as the start of the chicken ghost. And Beth Givens said she thought it was a slave killed trying to escape."

"Ah, that makes sense. I ran into Beth about an hour ago and she was trying to tell me something, but I get bored with her gossip and only half listen. Now that I think of it, she may have mentioned escaped slaves."

Ida threw out, "Do you know who Erin Byrnes is? You didn't seem to know yesterday, but did you sense or learn anything about her?"

Star sighed. "No, it's interesting you ask that. I did try

to do some research on the internet and I consulted some tea leaves. But I found nothing."

Ginger responded. "Well we did. Her married name is Erin Walsh and they say she was psychic."

Star went white. "*The* Erin Walsh?"

Ginger shrugged. "I don't know who *the* Erin Walsh is, but Erin Byrnes married a Conner Walsh."

Star's eyes were wide. "Erin Walsh was a legend in the south. It's impossible to be a medium and not run into stories about her. She supposedly could predict the future and it drove her mad."

Ida moaned. "Well this mystery is driving me crazy. How can a tiny locket cause so much trouble."

Star chuckled. "It's the littlest ripples that cause the biggest waves."

Ida pinched her eyebrows. "Why does everyone have to talk like Dumbledore today? Did someone put something in the water?" She took out her phone and opened the picture of the painting. "Star, does this mean anything to you?"

Star studied the image for a moment. "Maybe. The angels circling in the sky may mean a spirit is passing to heaven. But that's about it. It would help if I could see, or even touch, the original painting."

"Well, it's just across the street at the art gallery. Why not go have a look?" Once again, the question just slipped out of me. But I must have been right. All three woman looked at me like it was a revelation and without further discussion we made for the exit.

Chapter Ten

Star

The art gallery sits diagonally across the street from my New Age Store, but I somehow neglected to find a reason to visit. Today was different, I had a purpose so I flipped my sign to "Will Return Soon" and locked the front door. After which, Ginger led the way across Main Street to the recently opened gallery. As we entered, I sensed a presence.

Blanche said, "Oh, back so soon and the group is growing. Welcome, again."

Ginger smiled. "Thanks. We're as surprised as you, but Star wanted to see the painting in person."

Blanche smiled. "Of course. Can I get anyone something to drink? Water? And we do have some nice blackberry wine."

"No, I would like to see the painting. Is that it?" I pointed to a tripod near Blanche's two sisters, Cathy and Janis, who worked on the large piece of art it held.

Cathy bubbled, "Yes, we are restoring it for Dottie over at The Fluffy Pillow. This is your first time in the store, isn't it Star?"

"Yes, and it's nice to see Y'all." I approached the painting and the gleam was faint at first. With each step, though, the picture frame glowed brighter, lit by some unseen force. Stopping at arm's length from the canvas, light rays streamed in all directions. The colors morphed in a slow, seamless manner. This sight was stunning. Once, I encountered an object with a similar aura, but this was most impressive. I reached with my right hand to caress the frame, and as my fingertips grazed the old wood, the surge occurred.

Cold air flowed up from my feet until the chill engulfed my entire body. Then my muscles started to harden. As I resisted, my hands fell to my side but before long I froze like a statue. Time became irrelevant. However, while rigid, I experienced war. Not modern battle, but a montage displayed the brutality of muskets firing with old percussion caps, large deafening cannons, slaves scrambling to find freedom, wives and mothers wailing for lost husbands and sons, and buildings burning. Misery and suffering took up residence in every home in the land. Suddenly, the brutal war faded to white, followed by a serene scene that revealed a lone, beautiful woman sitting at a butter churn. She was dressed in a long brown hoop dress with a large white apron to protect the clothing. To protect her head, the woman wore a white bonnet. After sobbing for a while, she spoke to me, asking for compassion and understanding. I learned embarrassment brought her tears, but I failed to discern the cause.

And suddenly, I warmed, returning to reality. Ginger asked, "Star, are you all right?"

"Yeah. I think so." If being honest, I was unsure, but nothing hurt too much.

Bones grimaced at me and put his arm around my shoulders to console me. "That was freaky. You felt like a cold piece of steel when I tried to wake you up. I hugged and shook you to try and get you out of it. Here, have a seat."

Janis extended me a glass of wine but I shook my head no. "I would prefer water if you would be so kind." She took the glass away and left to get some water.

"Did you see anything. That was a trance if I ever saw one. You must have seen something." Ida's eyebrows raised more than usual.

"Yeah. But it was mostly war. Like the Civil War. Brutal." I still felt shock from the savage images observed. I forced my mind to think of the woman again. "But then it faded and I saw a beautiful woman. She sat with a butter churn."

Ginger snorted. "Like that?" She was pointing at the woman in the painting, who sat at a churn.

"It was something like that but the woman was more beautiful. The woman in the painting doesn't really look like the woman in my vision." My jaw hung when the thought flashed. "Ida, do you have the pictures from inside the locket on your phone."

Ida chuckled. "Of course. I always leave locked and loaded."

Blanche quipped. "And you leave your humility at home I see."

Ida answered the art curator with laser beams from her eyes. "It is a thin line between being cocky and being good."

Ginger threw her hands in the air. "Just show Star the pictures of the two people from the locket."

"Jeez, no one has a sense of humor anymore." Ida took a phone out, opened files, then handed the device to me.

I gasped. "It's her. This is the woman I saw in my vision."

Bones asked, "Is it the same woman in the painting though? Star, you said she looked different."

Blanche answered. "Sometimes a scene is painted depicting people after an event and the artist creates what he remembers the people to look like. It is not always a perfect recreation of how they look, so it could still be her."

Ginger sat next to me. "Star, is there anything else from this vision?"

After running what I remembered through my mind, it hit me. "Her, I saw her. This slave was in my vision fleeing for her life." I pointed to the figure in the painting.

Ida responded. "This is confusing. The butter woman doesn't match the vision, but this slave in the painting does. How can that be?"

Ginger added, "That's a new part of this mystery for us to figure out. But for now, I'm stumped. Does anyone else have theories?"

Cathy returned with the water and overheard the conversation. "In art, there is an interesting explanation and it is common to find something like this. The people who commission a painting are often depicted more accurately because the artist can see them, even have them model. But others that have to be recreated from memory…they can be painted, well, imperfect."

Ida pinched her eyebrows. "So the slave had the painting made?"

Cathy nodded. "Probably, if Star's vision is correct."

"How could a slave afford this? A painting like this back then must have been expensive." Ginger was thinking out loud.

Blanche answered her. "Some slaves who made it to freedom became wealthy. So if this was a scene that occurred during this slave's escape, she might have commissioned it years later and that is why the butter churner looks different. The butter churner would have been described to the artist by the slave. And the artist gave it his best shot."

Bones grunted. "Wow! Didn't think of that, but it makes sense."

Something was off and I said. "But why would a woman churning butter be the moment you want to capture during your flight to freedom?"

Ida looked at me like I just ripped off a large Band-Aid. "That…that's a good question."

Ginger locked onto my eyes. "Was there anything else in your vision to help answer that?"

I began sensing the paranormal when I was a little girl. The strange events disturbed me at first, but over time, I learned this was a gift and appreciated the secrets revealed by the supernatural. However, a downside existed. It concerned most people, including my parents, and resulted in an eccentric childhood. I was an outcast, an outsider…different. A few years ago, when I rented the space next to The Grumpy Chicken, for the first time I perceived a sense of belonging. Recent events proved me right; I ended up here for a reason. But my gifts still have the power to agitate me, and this recent trance shook my emotions. With some effort, I cleared my mind and forced calm. "Not really, Ginger. But maybe after I rest a little. It was pretty intense."

Ginger added, "Hey, have you eaten today? Maybe we can head over to the pub and get something for you to eat."

I shook my head no. "That's not necessary. I really should get back to work."

Ida said, "It's better for you to tell everyone. If we try to do it, it will be described wrong for sure. And with this crowd, that will just start some argument about something silly, like whether the butter she's churning tastes good or not."

Bones chuckled. "I saw it happen and I want to hear Star describe it. This was sooo weird."

I replied, "I should return to my shop."

Ginger smiled at me. "I understand, it's getting late anyway. Bones has to help Dad with the dinner crowd and I'm sure the kitchen is a wreck. But, the gang agreed to meet tomorrow for lunch. Piper and Digger will be back from Atlanta and we plan on sharing what we have all learned. Seems to me, you might want to be part of that, Star."

I smiled. "You're right. I will see ya at lunch tomorrow then."

Ginger spun to Blanche. "Do you know who painted this?" She pointed at the tripod as she spoke.

"No, not yet. But I suspect we will after we get the frame off." Blanche glanced at her two sisters to see if they agreed, and they nodded affirmatively. "I'll let you know what we find. Thanks for coming by."

Ginger waved. "Thanks. See ya for now."

We all waved goodbye and made for the exit to cross Main Street once again. The events of the day provided much to ponder and sleep would be difficult tonight. It also dawned on me, witnessing a trance was likely as dramatic as being in the trance. No one would get much shut-eye this night.

Chapter Eleven

Guardrail

Yesterday, Dog Breath and I worked late to finish a big custom motorcycle job so we would be the first ones in the pub today. Our business comes first, but it was time to join the fun.

Ida greeted us. "You're early. Did you miss being part of the flatfoot crowd?"

Dog muttered. "To be honest, yeah. Why should they get to have all the fun?"

"We can't ignore our customers. But it's a little unsettling to be left out of the sleuthing. So we figured we would get here early and grab a bite to eat. Be ready." I waved to Bones through the order window.

"Hey Guardrail, you should've been there yesterday. Star had a humdinger of a trance. And it was loaded with info." Bones had to yell so we could hear him.

Dog barked back, "Well, we're here now. Ready to rumble."

I smacked my partners arm. "Rumble? What are you talking about."

Dog smacked me back. "I can talk hip if I want."

Star sat at the bar talking to Dixie. She laughed and turned to Dog. "If that's your hip talk, I would just talk regular from now on." Her remark made me laugh.

Ginger came out of the kitchen. "Gentlemen, good to see you. What are you laughing at?"

I waved her off. "Nothing. You had to be here."

Ginger continued, "Well, you missed lots yesterday, glad you boys could make it today."

"We heard that you were poking around. And Beth Givens has been making the rounds, too. She knows something weird is going on but is going nuts not knowing the whole story." I took a seat on my stool.

Dog sat next to me and said, "So, what's going on? What did you found out?"

The spinster sisters interrupted as they entered through the front door. Edith raised her voice. "Good day! I see the gang is assembling." The sisters moved to their table and sat as they talked.

Ginger replied. "Yes, the gang is back together, just as planned. All we need now is Digger and…" The front door opened and revealed Digger. She continued, "Check that, we need Piper and Ida."

Digger took his stool and slouched. I asked, "What's your problem?"

"Well Guardrail, you ride for six hours with Piper and deal with a mad scientist for an entire day. Then see if you have to ask." Digger hung his head while speaking.

Ginger asked, "So, the trip went poorly?"

"No, I enjoyed some of it. I got to sign my first autograph. It was exciting." Digger picked his head upon mentioning the signature.

"I signed my first one not too long ago. It's strange when someone asks, but yeah, kind of exciting." Ginger smiled at the old gravedigger.

"I guess the ride to and from was OK, but that historian was a handful. He bounced all over the place and told some whoppers. And he kept looking at me like I was E.T."

I laughed and asked, "So, you weren't impressed with him, were ya Digger?"

He turned to look at me. "You could say that, Guardrail."

Ginger added, "Well, we'll have to see what Piper thought of him and what she learned."

We didn't have to wait long, Piper and Ida entered

with a surprise in tow. An energetic man in his sixties with flowing, bushy gray hair accompanied them. Piper said, "Back from the big city and we got news."

Dog shot back. "Who's this?" He pointed at the man with them.

Digger mumbled. "That's the handful."

I sensed my eyes grow large. "That's the historian?"

Digger nodded. "Yep!"

Edith and Lily sat up straight. Lily tittered, "Oh my, it's always so nice to welcome a handsome, young stranger. Here, come sit at our table."

Edith pulled out the chair next to her and patted the seat. "Come, sit here next to me."

Piper spoke up. "Everyone. This is Blake Winston from the Atlanta Historical Society. He's been very helpful. But this puzzle may be much larger than we suspected, so he asked to come back to Potter's Mill and continue researching the issue."

Ginger said, "You could have called, told us ahead of time."

"Why? Would it have made a difference? Thought I would surprise you." Piper grinned at Ginger. "I love when you make that astonished face."

Dog said, "Well if I got my count right, the gang's all here. We can start."

Ginger said, "OK. Who wants to go first?"

Bones yelled from the kitchen. "Star! The trance was incredible!"

Ginger said, "No. We have a guest. He should be allowed to go first. Blake, we're pleased to have you here. Can you tell us what you learned about the locket?"

Blake told the story of the locket inspection and presented his theory. He finished with, "The grumpy chicken is Lee's pet chicken, Nellie, and she is guarding the confederate's lost gold. And this locket bothered her because it puts the gold in jeopardy."

Dog laughed uncontrolled. "You can't be serious. The lost gold has been searched for over decades. And you want us to believe it's here." He wiped the tears from his eyes.

Edith reached out and touched his hand. "You have an interesting theory, dear. Maybe we can discuss it later over dinner. At my place."

Lily corrected. "It's our place! And we serve fine tea and cookies for dessert. Or whatever else you might like."

Piper intervened. "Ladies, if you please. Blake has an interesting theory and some of the facts fit."

I added, "But not all the facts fit. With everything that has happened with the chicken, no one has ever mentioned gold. Not even Star after a trance."

Star sat quietly but picked this point in the conversation to join. "Guardrail is right. I have never sensed the chicken is protecting something of value, like a gold treasure. In contrast, I sense embarrassment and a desire to make things right. To contribute and do good deeds."

Dog said, "So, the Atlanta visit turned up some interesting info. What about you, Ginger? You poked around town yesterday according to rumors. What did you find?"

Ginger shrugged, "Ida and Bones should tell you. They found the interesting stuff."

Ida cut in, "We found an old map in a trunk at Bessie Houston's house. It showed the pub on it but it used to be called the Fickle Waterwheel and was owned by the Walsh family."

"Maybe the pub should be called The Fickle Pickle. Seems sometimes we have pickled eggs, and sometimes we don't." I should have held my tongue.

Ginger glared at me. "This is not about the pickled egg jar problem, Guardrail. Bones also found some history of business conducted in the town back during the civil war in an old ledger."

Ida added, "And we noticed the scroll design on the map matched the scroll work on the locket. So they seem connected somehow."

Bones came out of the kitchen wiping his hands on a

white towel. "We also found an old letter from one of the Walsh sons who fought in the Civil War. He said that his mother's side of the family, the Byrnes, had a respectable military history."

Ida continued, "And at the end of the day we inspected an odd painting. Then after talking with Star, she wanted to see it. So we headed over to the art gallery and when she touched the frame, well things got freaky."

Blake cut in, "We're overlooking two important facts. Everything we learned confirms Erin Walsh was Erin Byrnes before she married. This is significant. And if the scroll work on a map matches the engraving on the locket, that is highly unusual."

Ginger nodded. "Good points."

I interrupted. "Wait, so what went on in the art gallery? When you touched the frame, Star, what happened?"

Star drew a deep breath. "I froze and saw the Civil War being fought. Then it faded to a woman churning butter. She spoke to me and she was crying because she was embarrassed."

Blake asked, "What was she embarrassed about?"

Lily sat up straight whispered to him. "Oh, that is such a smart question, Mr. Winston."

Star shrugged. "I came out of the trance before I found out. But the woman in my vision was the woman in the locket. And one of the escaping slaves I saw was in the painting."

Dog Breath blinked uncontrolled. "What? How could you see the woman in the locket? And what slave?"

Ida chuckled. "There's a painting in the art gallery across the street and it shows a woman churning butter talking to a group of slaves."

Dog added, "You left that part out. That makes more sense."

I chuckled, "I have to admit, there are quite a few pieces to this puzzle and I'm getting confused myself, partner."

Blake asked, "Do you have the map here?"

Ida replied. "Yep."

The historian continued. "May I please see it?"

Ida laid the map on the bar with care. It had deep creases from the long storage and she rubbed the folds gently to coax it flat. "So, Digger, you still have the locket?" He nodded yes and she continued. "So, get it out and let's see how good a match it is. I only had pictures to compare with yesterday."

Digger moved over to the map and laid the locket on the old piece of paper. Two things happened when the necklace touched the old map.

"SQUAAAAAK!!!!"

A long wail emanated from the ceiling that sounded like a cross of a woman's voice and chicken's squawk. We all jumped and looked around as if to see the chicken ghost among us. Then, a faint spot of light glowed, as if a small LED light was shining beneath the map. Digger gasped. "That's the cemetery where I work. And I know this spot. The grass grows different there and neither bird nor animal tread there. It's rumored to be the grave of a witch."

Blake gushed. "Look close, you can make out the name Walsh as a small watermark under the glowing spot. We must go there, see why the map pointed to this particular spot."

Edith swooned. "So brave. I knew it when I first laid eyes you."

Digger cut off Edith. "I'll take ya, Mr. Historian, but only in broad daylight. We can go right after I finish my lunch. Things can get weird in the cemetery at night, especially at that spot."

Chapter Twelve

Digger

The historian kept asking questions while I tried to enjoy my burger and beer. It was obvious that I needed to make this trip to the cemetery immediately. Or Blake would talk me to death.

Blake babbled. "It could mean just about anything, but the most obvious is the Confederate gold is buried there. Why else would the scroll work of a famous Civil War-era New York City jeweler be on a map of Potter's Mill?"

I snapped. "Don't you ever stop talking?"

The old historian flinched. "I'm sorry, I didn't realize I was irritating you."

"I'm not sure irritating is a strong enough word." I glared at him.

Ginger laughed. "I see you two aren't destined to be best friends, maybe someone else should go with you to the cemetery."

The spinster sisters both perked up. Edith spoke. "We would gladly accompany Blake to the cemetery."

Ginger shook her head no. "This may involve digging. I think we should send a young, strong body."

The swinging door from the kitchen flew open. Bones sprinted out and I think he attempted to make his chest appear bigger. The young grill cook said, "I can go and I'm good at digging."

"Well, if there is digging to do, I think I can handle it. My name is Digger after all."

Ginger added, "Digger, I know, but it would be good for Bones to help. Make it easier for you to deal with whatever else you find. And on that point, maybe someone else should go to help document things. Like Piper."

Piper choked on her lunch. After clearing her throat, she replied. "Oh no, I'm not a cemetery kind of girl."

Ginger squinted. "But you're a journalist. Don't you want the story?"

Piper snorted. "Sure, but I'll report this story as told by eyewitnesses."

Ida spoke. "I'll go. I have cameras and I can check things online remotely, both of which may help."

Blake added. "I have my camera too. But if you can get internet access remotely, that would be useful."

Ginger slapped the bar. "It's settled. The cemetery recon team is Ida, Digger, Bones, and Blake."

Lily ogled the newcomer. "Blake, please be careful."

I heard enough. "For crying out loud. Let's just get this over with. Is everyone ready to go?"

Ida and Bones nodded yes. Blake just stared at me. He finally said, "I'm not sure. I may need equipment."

"We have everything we need. If you find you need something else, we can always go back when you get your gear."

Blake agreed and we made for the exit. Unsurprising, Blake talked the whole time as we walked. "We think the remote location and unusual paranormal activity made Bear's Paw Swamp the perfect location to hide the Confederate gold. But the other historians and I argue all the time over who owns the gold and what do they want to do with it?"

Ida interrupted. "You're so sure about this treasure, but what if the gold isn't there? Aren't you scientist types supposed to have an open mind?"

"Yes. But nothing stops us from having hope, too." Blake smiled at her.

I pointed. "There it is. The only plot in the place where the grass grows short and yellow. And all the animals avoid the spot."

Blake power walked over to the plot. He scanned the

area and spun to me. "Digger, can we excavate?"

I rubbed my chin. "Maybe. It's only a rumor that this is a witch's burial site, so it's not officially a grave."

Bones said, "Where do you keep the shovels. No sense wasting time." I pointed to the work shed and Bones made a beeline. After a couple of minutes, he returned and smiled at me. "I got us both a shovel. I know digging here can be tough, so I grabbed some extra help." Bones held up a pickax to show me.

Bones manned one shovel and me the other. We dug, for an hour, till my shovel made a solid thud on what was unmistakably a piece of wood. I stopped and knelt for a closer look. It was a small chest.

Blake gasped. "It's the gold!"

Bones smiled and Ida must have broken her jaw to hang so low. Ida gathered herself and whipped out her phone. "Let me get some pictures to document this. This could be a major find."

I removed the chest from the hole and placed on a flat patch of grass. Blake studied the old box and said, "This is so beautiful. Look at the blacksmith work on the lock and hinges. And the wood seems to be yew. Makes sense if it was intended to be buried."

Bones exclaimed, "Open it."

Blake responded, "That's just it, the lock is unusual and it has no keyhole. I can't open it."

"Here let me see." I did not trust this old microscope jockey. But he was right, I did not find a way to open the lock.

Ida said, "We should take this back to the pub. Let everyone have a look and see if we can figure out how to open it."

Bones nodded yes, Blake stared at her, and I said, "Not yet, there may be more in the dirt."

Blake's eyes widened. "You're right. We should keep digging for a bit, make sure we don't miss something."

Bones and I jumped back in the hole and dug until the blisters and sweat told us we went deep enough. At that point, we were certain the chest was the only thing buried. It was time to return to the pub. We climbed out of the hole and headed for The Grumpy Chicken with the chest.

Blake again tried to domineer the talk on the way back. But this time, he had competition. Ida and Bones chattered and kept him from controlling the conversation. We walked back into the pub to find a large, but quiet crowd.

"What happened here?" I rarely found the pub this quiet.

Ginger answered, "We're not sure, Digger. About an hour ago, the grumper went mad. Some of the usual stuff she does to cause trouble. But this time Star blacked out and the dancing giant returned. The thuds of his feet cracked some tiles. Look!" She pointed at a spot on the floor.

Dixie exclaimed, "And we saw the chicken! She was just a reflection in the mirror. But me and Ginger saw her."

Star sat a dining table appearing weary. I sat next to her. "Are you okay, Star?" I placed the chest on the dining table.

"I'm not sure. I never blacked out like that and I feel like I have a hangover."

Edith and Lily raced over to Blake. Lily gushed, "It was horrible. The thuds from the floor shook the room and we thought Star was dead." She hugged him. "Are you alright?"

Blake tried to pry Lily off. "I'm fine. Does this kind of thing happen here a lot?"

Dixie yelled back at him from the bar, "More than ya know!"

The historian raised his eyebrows. "That's kind of disturbing."

Lily realized I carried something. She asked, "Digger, what's that?"

"Obviously a chest. But we can't open it to see what's inside."

Guardrail hollered, "The gold?"

"Nope, I don't think so. It's too light." I knew after carrying it back from the cemetery.

Ginger examined the old box. "This lock is so unusual. But we need to open it."

Dog Breath cut in. "I know someone who might be able to help."

In unison, we all shot back, "Who?"

Dog replied, "Elias Holland."

Ginger gasped. "Elias? Why him?"

Dog shrugged. "He's smart, good with this kind of thing. Everyone thinks he just knows gaming, but he is good with mechanical things, too. But I seem to be the only one who actually talks to him when he comes in here."

Ginger sighed. "I don't know. He's kept pretty much to himself since that business with his Mom's death. It seems like a long shot."

Dog Breath scanned the crowd. "It's just an idea. Does anyone have a better one?"

The room fell silent.

Ida chuckled. "Well, that's just what we need, someone else involved in this. But not just another person, the slightly unstable son whose mom was murdered by her money-grubbing fifth husband. And don't forget *her* first four husbands all died under mysterious circumstances. Yeah, Elias sounds like the guy we need right now."

Ginger raised her eyebrows and studied Ida. "Wow, that was a mouthful. Were you channeling Dixie?"

Dixie complained. "Hey, don't lump me into that. I think Dog had a good idea."

Blake spoke meekly. "I have some resources, too. I can send pictures of the chest, see if they know anything or have any ideas." His voice trailed off.

Dixie chuckled and ignored the historian. "Hey, let's send Digger to fetch Elias at the cat house. We all know how much he likes cats."

Ginger smiled. "That's the Dixie I know."

I glared at Dixie. "Over my dead body!"

Blake's face went long and his eyes grew wide. "I am starting to think you're all slightly off."

Piper laughed. "Nah, that's just the way it is in The Grumpy Chicken. You get used to the ghost chicken after a while."

Blake took a stool at the bar. "I think I need a sherry if you would be so kind."

Dixie snorted. "Sherry huh? We don't serve that very often. Let me see if we still have a bottle."

Blake produced a phone and made calls while he

sipped the sherry. At the same time, the group chose Dog Breath for the task of visiting Elias and asking for help. And with that, the effort was on to open the chest.

Chapter Thirteen

Dog Breath

It is hard for me to blend, but I worked on improving my social skills over the years. Guardrail nicknamed me Dog Breath, despite my objections, and the why is a long story. But he is my best friend and business partner, so he gets me better than most.

The others are oblivious to the mental damage that two tours in Vietnam do to a person. Even Guardrail is unaware at times of the anguish I carry from those years. However, they accept me as a member of the group. They are my family and their support is invaluable. Plus I love the mysteries we investigate, maybe a little too much.

I made the short walk to the Holland house and found Elias home. On cracking the door, he said, "Hey Dog Breath."

"Hello, Elias. We haven't seen you in the pub in a while."

He sighed. "I know. But I haven't been in a real social mood after the troubles. But thanks for coming by."

"You're welcome. But I'm afraid I'm here on business. We have a problem you might be able to help us with. It has to do with the chicken ghost."

Elias chuckled. "I don't believe in the grumpy chicken. You know that. But what's your problem?"

"We found a chest with a weird lock and maybe you can help us open it."

Elias tilted his head. "Didn't expect something like that. Why do you think I can help?"

"Because there is no keyhole. It is a mechanical puzzle and you are good with that kind of stuff."

"Locks with no keyhole tend to have a trigger, like a magnetic key, or a hidden latch. And did you examine the hinges? The keyhole may be on the hinge. That is a trick I learned from a friend in a chat room. And of course, there is the old deception of a hidden drawer or a secret door to the inside"

I smiled. "See, I came to the right person. We have some smart people back at the pub, including a professor from Atlanta, and none of them thought of that."

"Wow, so this is a big mystery if you have experts

from Atlanta in town."

"Yeah, his visit just kind of happened, like most things around here. But this chest is a doozy of a brain-teaser. I appreciate your input."

"No problem. After you try my suggestions, let me know if you can't get it open. Maybe I'll come on over then."

"Thanks, I will if we need you. Take care."

Elias smiled and closed the door. I turned and started my return trip by navigating around all the cats as I marched down the front walk. During the walk back, I thought of how Elias endured his mother's murder and understood that he preferred to stay at home. Even the offer to come down to the pub was a big deal for him. Perhaps his mental wounds are healing.

I was back soon enough and reentered the pub, taking my usual stool. Everyone silently stared at me. "What!"

Ginger spoke. "Well, glad you made it back, Dog. But where is Elias?"

"He didn't want to come. But he had a couple of ideas. He said there may be a magnetic latch or that the lock is actually disguised as one of the hinges. Oh, and that we should look for a secret door." A beer appeared in front of me. "Thanks, Dixie."

Blake said, "An expert in Denver said something similar. He told me to look for a sliding panel or secret drawer."

"So did you look?" I took a sip of beer and stared at the odd scientist while waiting for my answer.

Blake jerked back. "Of course, but I found nothing."

Ida had moved to the chest, which still sat on the dining table in front of Star. After hearing my comments, Ida inspected the hinges. She carefully probed the metal with her fingers and said, "I think this one is different."

Blake asked, "Why?"

Ida continued, "It looks the same as the other hinge, but it doesn't sound as solid when I tap it with my fingernail."

Blake went to the chest to try for himself. His eyebrows rose. "Dang! You're right. There is something different with this hinge. Piper, can I have the keys to your car? I have some tools in my travel bag."

Piper threw him the keys and Blake left to retrieve the needed items. Piper laughed. "Who has tools in their overnight bag."

Digger volleyed back, "A flaky historian."

Piper chuckled. "You promoted Blake from a handful to flaky."

Digger stared at his beer. "No, just showing off my limited vocabulary."

Blake returned with a small toolbox. He opened it and

took out a jeweler's loop. After examining the suspect hinge with magnification, he said, "I think this is the latch. It has some expertly crafted cavities shaped like a heart. They could be tiny screw drives for a specialized screwdriver. One with a tiny heart-shaped tip to fit the socket."

Digger snorted. "Where are we going to find a screwdriver like that?" He patted a pocket to confirm the locket was still safe.

Blake saw him feel for the trinket and asked, "Can it be? Digger, can I see the locket again?"

Digger glared at the historian but eventually handed it to the historian. Blake studied it with the magnifying loop. "How did I miss this. I guess it wasn't hard. It's in the hinge and we never really studied the hinge under the microscope." With the locket closed, he slid a finger along the spine of the small hinge. A tiny wire protruded from the hinge. "So beautiful, and clever."

Dixie snorted. "That has to be the oldest James Bond style device ever."

Blake smiled. "You may be more right than you know."

He carefully took the exposed, minuscule screwdriver sticking out of the locket hinge and held it to the larger chest hinge.

The air went cold, the lights flickered, the chicken wailed. "SQUAAAAAAK!!!"

All the usual grumpy chicken temper tantrum tricks. But this time the chest floated off the table a foot into the air and spun, slowly. Then it continued to rise. Blake reacted to the movement and jumped onto it, holding tight. He spun with the chest, the rotations increasing steadily. A blood-curdling "NO!!!" reverberated before Blake and the chest crashed back to the floor.

Guardrail chuckled. "What do you think, Dog? That was either really stupid or really brave."

I added, "Riding a floating chest? My money is on stupid."

Blake stared at the two of us with blurry eyes. Piper helped him up and into a chair. She got a wet cloth and wiped his face. Blake protested. "Stop. I'm fine, I'm just a bit stunned. I have never seen anything like that. It was incredible."

Piper snickered. "You're a regular now, I think."

Blake scanned the area where he fell. He panicked. I learned why when he got down on his hands and knees and retrieved the locket. Blake glanced at Digger. "It's alright. Nothing broken."

Digger glared at the old historian, quiet and motionless. Then he gave a slight nod to Blake. The historian understood and resumed his work. This time, he placed the chest on the bar in front of him so he could work standing. Once again, he held the tiny screwdriver protruding from the locket hinge and worked at the trick chest hinge. With caution, he used the small tool and in less than a minute, the hinge popped open like a latch. He exclaimed, "Voila!"

Everyone gathered around with the chest on the verge of revealing its contents. Dixie blurted out, "We need Geraldo Rivera like when he did that special with Al Capone's safe."

Ginger chuckled. "No way. He found that safe empty. I want to find something inside this puppy."

Blake continued to play with the chest top. "It appears that once this hinge is released, it is still a bit of a puzzle. I need to find the right way to twist or slide the top…" The lid rotated off to one side exposing the contents.

Ginger approached the open chest and reached. Blake grabbed her hand. "No, wait. You need to put gloves on. And be very gentle. This is very old and fragile. And it may be one of the more important finds from the Civil War."

Blake produced two sets of rubber gloves from his toolkit. He gave Ginger one set and put the other on his own hands. Once she had the gloves on, they proceeded. Blake laid out a clean towel and removed the first item. It was a quilt square and a second fabric square followed. He placed them both gently on the towel. Ginger was busy removing an envelope from the chest. Her peepers were so wide I thought her eyeballs might fall out.

Then we all spied it. The glint of gold is hard to miss.

Coins sprinkled the bottom of the chest.

Blake moved his stare from face to face, around the room. "It's not the Confederate gold, but this is a significant find."

Chapter Fourteen

Ginger

The chest produced an envelope with a handwritten letter, two quilt squares, and fourteen gold coins. Blake hovered over the fabric pieces. "These are quilt codes. The underground railroad used them to pass messages. You see, the patterns had meaning. In the locket, there is a photo of a man. I assume he is Conner Walsh and he is wearing a pin with that also depicts a quilt code. Then we find a chest with a letter from him and two quilt squares displaying known coded messages." He picked one up. "This one is the monkey wrench. It means to gather the tools needed for your escape. The other one is called the drunkard's path. It tells the fleeing slaves to take a zigzag path to evade the pursuers and their hounds. These are pieces of history. But all together they tell me Conner Walsh worked the underground railroad. He may have even been a conductor."

Digger asked, "What's a conductor on the underground railroad?"

"Someone who guided the escaped slaves along the way."

Guardrail asked, "So this underground railroad was real, and Potter's Mill was part of it?"

Blake bubbled, "Yes, well technically the underground railroad was a concept, not a place. But it appears Conner Walsh may have been a key player in operating it."

Dog Breath cut in, "Wow! So what happened to the Walsh family?"

Blake spun to face him, "Good question. If I remember right, Conner and Erin Walsh had five children, two boys and three girls. Both sons were killed in the Civil War, meaning the name was lost when the three girls married and changed their last names."

"So are any of us descendants still in town?" For some reason, I feared the answer to that question, but the history was too interesting to ignore.

Blake smiled at me. "That is another good question, Ginger, and as the owner of an old pub, I am sure you want to know. But I have to defer to others back in Atlanta who are doing some work to follow up on our findings."

The envelope seemed unimportant next to the gold coins and the historically significant quilt squares. But I needed to know what it contained. I picked it up, lifted the flap and removed a three-page letter. It was handwritten and hard to read, but I read it out loud.

To Winny Carter,

The Conner family sincerely regrets a misunderstanding when on one fateful day you approached my wife Erin, who churned butter in a field and you asked for her help in Bear's Paw Swamp. According to my wife, she froze and did not know what to do. The barking of dogs drove you off before she could collect her wits. Your group of five surprised her in broad daylight, in view of others. We worked so hard to keep the railroad secret, and please, believe me, Erin wanted to help. She told me that night about the incident and I promised to look for your group the next day.

But the next day, General Sherman sacked our town, burning it all to the ground. My wife, Erin, was killed as she raced into a burning barn to save our horses. The loss was devastating to me as my only two sons were also lost in the war. I forgot the incident with you for years and tried to get on with life.

We eventually rebuilt our town, including the pub owned and managed by one of my daughters. When the pub reopened, almost immediately the strange occurrences began. Soon, rumors started that the place was haunted, and even worse, the ghost was said to be my wife Erin.

A few years later, I learned of a story. A ship's captain told me about a slave who encountered a woman churning butter on her way to Savannah. The incident with you the day before Erin's death came flooding back.

This slave further told the sea captain that she ran from New Orleans and she was a Voodoo priestess. And as the pursuing dogs barked, she fled from a butter churner who she cursed to spend an eternity as a coward, experiencing life in chains for not lending help. After hearing this tale, my daughter saw the ghost haunting the new pub and it was a chicken wearing a shackle. I believe this strange yarn as true, and my beloved wife, Erin, has been forced to spend eternity as a chicken wearing a shackle.

I have sought the Voodoo priestess for years and my research indicates that you are the slave from that day who applied this wretched curse. Enclosed are two quilt pieces used by Erin and me as proof that we served to assist many fleeing slaves on their way to Savannah. This was a misunderstanding and you mistook my wife's fear of witnesses for not wanting to help you.

I was pleased to learn you made it all the way to New England and I am happy that you have found success in life. Now, years after war's end and emancipation, I ask for your forgiveness and implore you, please lift this horrible curse. As I understand the situation, you are the only one who can remove the hex and let my wife rest in peace. I beg that you hear my plea and let my family find harmony after the sufferings of war. For your trouble, I have enclosed an advanced payment as a sign of my true intentions to make peace with you.

Truthfully yours,

Conner T. Walsh

Treasurer, Bear's Paw Swamp

I felt the tear trickle down my cheek. The grumpy chicken was part of my life since birth. But never did I ever suspect it was a woman cursed to this existence.

Blake said, "This is incredible. I was so sure the chicken ghost of yours was Nellie, General Lee's pet chicken. But to find it is Erin Byrnes, this is incredible."

Dog Breath chided, "So you believe in ghosts now, do ya, Blake?"

Blake laughed. "You're asking the man who just did a bucking bull ride on top of a whirling, floating chest."

Dog chuckled. "Good point."

The letter attracted Star. She approached me and took it, exhaling as she ran her fingers over the words. "This was written with so much love."

Blake asked, "Star, you should not be touching that with your fingers. The oils will damage it." The historian scanned the contents. "I need to bring all this back to Atlanta, for further analysis. Is that a problem?"

Digger rose off the stool and turned red. "It is. The locket was given to me by the spirits. And I found the chest. It's mine."

Blake countered. "Technically, it is the property of the Walsh family, clearly intended as a gift to the Carter family."

Guardrail bellowed, "Look, we need some time to figure this out. So let's all just have a seat and enjoy a nice cold beer. And maybe we can discuss what happened to the Walsh family. Seems to me their descendants might have something to say about all this too."

"You're right. If this story is true, and I can't believe I'm going to say it, but I do believe it to be real, the Walsh family is entitled to this letter at a minimum, and probably the quilt squares and chest. I don't know about the gold coins."

Piper shot a compassionate look over to Star and me. "Ginger has a point. Besides, we aren't going to do much more today, it's getting late in the day. We can use a little more time talking this through. Our adrenaline is still flowing with everything that has happened today."

Dixie was uncharacteristically quiet but broke her

silence. "My head feels funny. Did we just learn who our feathered poltergeist is?"

Bones sneaked out of the kitchen and leaned on the end of the bar. "I can't believe Tom went to Mae's for the day. He missed all of this." The skinny cook shook his head. "You know, something is still bothering me, why didn't the grumpy chicken go nuts when we read the letter or took the contents out of the chest?"

Star spoke. "I thought of that too, Bones. But she did protest when we tried to open the chest. It was her last attempt to keep her secret safe. Outbursts like that take a lot out of a spirit."

Bones asked, "But why is it such a big secret?"

Star continued, "Erin feels she brought shame to her family. And who wants to let others know they are now an eternal chicken wearing a shackle? It also makes sense that I feel a need in her to help others. She wants to make things right whenever she can. And to protect her family."

Blake laughed. "That brings us back to the big question. Who is her family now? We need to find out what the researchers in Atlanta discovered. I would guess there are a number of Walsh descendants still in Potter's Mill. A bit of work remains to be done."

Blake took out his phone and made a number of phone calls. Ida went to work connecting to the net and downloading files, photographs, old news articles, and other miscellaneous materials from the researchers. She said, "This is a lot of stuff. I can print it out or send copies to other people's phones. But we are going to need to all pitch in to the go through all of this."

Piper made a long face. "This is going to be a long night."

I laughed. "I guess that means we should get started."

Guardrail said, "Ida's right. Let's divide and conquer."

Dog downed the last of his beer. "This is not the kind of investigative work I like, but oh well."

Bones jumped at the chance to help. Lily and Edith took the hard job of swooning over Blake.

Chapter Fifteen

Ginger

Three days passed after opening the chest and Blake Winston returned to Atlanta, to the dismay of Edith and Lily. The research team that he put together back at the historical society was excellent, but it still took us two full days to piece all the family lines together. And we only did enough to figure out how to handle the ownership issues with the chest and its contents, the locket, and the painting. It seems this little town contained many families over the years.

Piper and I returned to the pub after a quick trip to the general store. Dad was in the dining room repairing the broken tiles. After sneaking up behind him, I said, "You missed a spot with the grout."

Without looking up, Dad said, "Then grab some grout and give me a hand."

I folded my arms. "I don't know, I just found out I

own fourteen gold coins. And I am related to the Hollands, they have money and influence."

Dad chuckled. "Only you could find Civil War history that shows we and the Hollands are direct descendants of the Walsh family."

Piper said, "It's an interesting story. It always amazes me how things like that get lost over time, how people forget."

Digger was at the bar eating lunch. "I said right off, the lady in the locket looked a little like you, Ginger. And she turns out to be your great, great, great, I don't know how many greats are needed, grandmother."

I turned to look at him. "I know. It's strange to know. I feel different somehow after learning the truth."

Dad stood up and said, "About that. I need to talk to you. In private."

I shrugged. "Okay."

Dad yelled. "Bones, I need you to come out here and finish this tiling for me."

Bones answered, hollering through the order window. "Are you kidding. I got the kitchen to cover."

Digger rose from his stool. "Here, let me. You go talk to your daughter." Dad studied him to see if he was serious. Digger continued, "I've done a fair amount of tile work. I can handle this."

Dad told Digger, "Don't mess it up." And then he led me up into the apartment over the pub. This was unusual. We went into the small kitchen and made coffee. Dad said, "I can't believe I missed all the fun. I picked the one day that gold coins are found in an actual buried chest to go visit Mae."

I snorted. "It was different. I know this is going to sound weird, but I feel different after all this. The gang has been through a lot, even solved murders, but somehow this incident leaves me feeling changed."

Dad sighed. "Here, have a seat." He pulled out a chair and placed a cup of coffee in front of me. This was not like him and I remained standing, staring at my father. He pointed to the chair. "You will want to sit to hear this. Sit."

I sat. "I'm not sure what is going on here. If you were a woman I would swear you were going to tell me you're pregnant."

Dad laughed. "I have dreaded this day for a long time. Even more than the birds and the bees talk. But I need to tell you something. Something much more difficult to explain than being pregnant."

I gulped. "You can talk to me about anything. You know that."

Dad looked at his shoes. "I know. But this has to do with your mother."

My heart went from calm to heart attack in one beat.

"What is it, Dad?"

The pause was unbearable. He finally spoke. "Your Mom knew things. She could sense things. All the women in our family can."

"Well, Mom always knew the right thing to do. How to make things better."

Dad doctored his coffee with some cream. "Yes, she did. And so do you. Like I said, the women in our family have the ability to know things that other people don't. Our family has always been a sort of caretaker for this town. It is our fate, our destiny."

My head hurt processing the meaning of what he was telling me. "I have asked a number of times why I always seem to be in the middle of things."

Dad nodded. "Yes, I know. But I knew that's how it was supposed to be, that you are meant to help right the wrongs, help others in need."

"That makes it sound weird."

He chuckled. "I know. But it gets even stranger. Your mom would tell me that the grumper gave her clues, too. That her spirit always watched out for the town's people, but this spirit needed your mom's help to do it. Do you think it is random that Dixie and Bones work here? They needed help and we gave it to them. Dog Breath came home from Vietnam with PTSD and your mother helped him readjust. Almost everyone in town was helped by your mom at one time or another, with the grumper's insight."

I pushed the coffee away. "You know, around most kitchen tables this would be crazy talk. But I think I understand. The chicken has been cryptic with me sometimes, but it always pointed me in the right direction. To do the right thing."

Dad played with his spoon. "For decades, our family has been the pub owners and we filled this role of caretaker for the townsfolk. But over that time we forgot how it came to be. Why we were charged with this task. Somehow, the chicken chose this time, chose you, to reveal that history. You have learned far more about the grumper than your mother ever did. It is quite impressive."

For some reason, tears rolled down my face. "I miss Mom so much. But this knowledge, this connection our family has with the supernatural, makes it feel like her spirit is here with us, too."

Dad's eyes watered. "That makes me happy and sad all at once to hear you say that."

I laughed. It made the tears drip from my face. "I think I would have preferred if you told me you were pregnant."

"Wait here." Dad went into his bedroom for a minute then returned with an envelope. "It seems this is your week for old letters." He handed me the envelope. "Your mom asked I give this to you when it was time. She said I would know when that was. And I think it's time. It explains her experiences, what she learned about the grumpy chicken. It's more important to this town than people think. Now you are the connection between that pesky ghost foul and the town."

I stared at the letter, unable to move. "This is hard to process. How many people know about this?"

"You, me, and Mae. That's it."

The tears returned as I picked up the envelope and spotted Mom's handwriting. "I don't think I want to read this right now."

Dad laughed. "You don't have to. After this week, I think you know more about the chicken than anyone ever has. Read it when you are ready."

I rose and went over to Dad and gave him a big hug. "I love you, Dad. And you don't have to say it back."

Dad hugged me back. "Sweetie, I love you more than anything in this universe. But if you tell anyone I said that I will deny it and throw something at you."

I laughed and kissed him on the cheek. "We should get back to the bar. Make sure Digger isn't creating a trip hazard and check that Bones isn't burning something under the salamander."

We both collected ourselves and we left the apartment to return to the pub. Piper saw us coming down the stairs. "Hey, Ginger. Blake called. The historical society liked my idea. They are going to help me set up a historical society here in town. And I am going to be the town historian. Our centerpiece displays are going to be the chest, the quilt squares, the painting and the locket we found."

"Just what we need, to give you more responsibility."

Piper laughed, "And to think I was going to ask you to be my assistant."

Dixie asked, "Ginger, what happened with the gold coins?"

"I asked Blake to see if he can locate the Carter family. Conner Walsh wanted to pay Winny Carter and it seems the coins are hers, well her family's now. So, I'm waiting to hear what he finds."

Dixie continued, "And how did Winny Carter's painting make it the Potter's Mill?"

I shrugged. "Don't know. That is one part of the mystery that remains unsolved. But Dottie agreed to let the historical society display it here in town."

Bones hollered from the kitchen. "So, you think the chicken is gone?"

"I doubt it. The grumpy chicken has been part of this place for a long time."

Bones hollered back. "Yeah, but now we know her secret."

I smiled. "I don't know, Bones, I think she still has a few secrets to keep."

The lights flickered, just once. Dixie murmured, "You don't think… Once means yes, right Ginger?"

"Yep. At least I think so."

Dad started waving his arms in the air. "Alright, everyone get back to work. This jibber jabber is out of control." He knelt down next to Digger fixing the tiles. "And you're… Actually, you're doing a good job. Keep going."

Our routines were returning, but the air inside the pub felt thick. Things were different. Change can be hard to accept and I would have to wait to see what the future revealed.

The End

Thanks for Reading! I hope you enjoyed the book and it would mean so much to me if you could leave a review. Reviews help authors gain more exposure and keep us writing your favorite stories.

You can find all of my books by visiting my Author Page.

Sign up for Constance Barker's New Releases Newsletter where you can find out when my next book is coming out and for special discounted pricing.

I never share or sell your email.

Visit me on Facebook and give me feedback on the characters and their stories.

Catalog of Books

The Grumpy Chicken Irish Pub Series

A Frosty Mug of Murder

Treachery on Tap

A Highball and a Low Blow

The Chronicles of Agnes Astor Smith

The Peculiar Case of Agnes Astor Smith

The Peculiar Case of the Red Tide

The Peculiar Case of the Lost Colony

Old School Diner Cozy Mysteries

Murder at Stake

Murder Well Done

A Side Order of Deception

Murder, Basted and Barbecued

The Curiosity Shop Cozy Mysteries

The Curious Case of the Cursed Spectacles

The Curious Case of the Cursed Dice

The Curious Case of the Cursed Dagger

The Curious Case of the Cursed Looking Glass

The We're Not Dead Yet Club

Fetch a Pail of Murder

Wedding Bells and Death Knells

Murder or Bust

Pinched, Pilfered and a Pitchfork

A Hot Spot of Murder

Witchy Women of Coven Grove Series

The Witching on the Wall

A Witching Well of Magic

Witching the Night Away

Witching There's Another Way

Witching Your Life Away

Witching You Wouldn't Go

Witching for a Miracle

Teasen & Pleasen Hair Salon Series

A Hair Raising Blowout

Wash, Rinse, Die

Holiday Hooligans

Color Me Dead

False Nails & Tall Tales

Caesar's Creek Series

A Frozen Scoop of Murder (Caesars Creek Mystery Series Book One)

Death by Chocolate Sundae (Caesars Creek Mystery Series Book Two)

Soft Serve Secrets (Caesars Creek Mystery Series Book Three)

Ice Cream You Scream (Caesars Creek Mystery Series Book Four)

Double Dip Dilemma (Caesars Creek Mystery Series Book Five)

Melted Memories (Caesars Creek Mystery Series Book Six)

Triple Dip Debacle(Caesars Creek Mystery Series Book Seven)

Whipped Wedding Woes(Caesars Creek Mystery Series Book Eight)

A Sprinkle of Tropical Trouble(Caesars Creek Mystery Series Book Nine)

A Drizzle of Deception(Caesars Creek Mystery Series Book Ten)

Sweet Home Mystery Series

Creamed at the Coffee Cabana (Sweet Home Mystery Series Book One)

A Caffeinated Crunch (Sweet Home Mystery Series Book Two)

A Frothy Fiasco (Sweet Home Mystery Series Book Three)

Punked by the Pumpkin(Sweet Home Mystery Series Book Four)

Peppermint Pandemonium(Sweet Home Mystery Series Book Five)

Expresso Messo(Sweet Home Mystery Series Book Six)

A Cuppa Cruise Conundrum(Sweet Home Mystery Series Book Seven)

The Brewing Bride(Sweet Home Mystery Series Book Eight)

Whispering Pines Mystery Series

A Sinister Slice of Murder

Sanctum of Shadows (Whispering Pines Mystery Series)

Curse of the Bloodstone Arrow (Whispering Pines Mystery Series)

Fright Night at the Haunted Inn (Whispering Pines Mystery Series)

Mad River Mystery Series

A Wicked Whack

A Prickly Predicament

A Malevolent Menace

40153049R00083

Made in the USA
Columbia, SC
12 December 2018